100 Reasons to Celebrate

We invite you to join us in celebrating Mills & Boon's centenary. Gerald Mills and Charles Boon founded Mills & Boon Limited in 1908 and opened offices in London's Covent Garden. Since then, Mills & Boon has become a hallmark for romantic fiction, recognised around the world.

We're proud of our 100 years of publishing excellence, which wouldn't have been achieved without the loyalty and enthusiasm of our authors and readers.

Thank you!

Each month throughout the year there will be something new and exciting to mark the centenary, so watch for your favourite authors, captivating new stories, special limited edition collections…and more!

Dear Reader

I'm delighted my current title, THE MARTINEZ MARRIAGE REVENGE, is being released in the year Mills & Boon celebrates its 100th birthday.

I read my first Mills & Boon romance when I was twelve, becoming spellbound by the characters, the romance, and even then I made up stories in my head… always romance, of course!

A budding author? Well, that didn't occur until I was married and housebound with three very young children! But there was never any doubt Mills & Boon would be the publisher to whom I'd submit!

My first book was published by Mills & Boon in 1975, and I value being part of their publishing history.

I adore the process of creating characters, exploring a theme, and bringing the story to life. Each book becomes a fascinating voyage of discovery as the characters' personalities develop, and their emotional reaction to each other evolves into everlasting love. Set partly in Perth, and mostly in Madrid, THE MARTINEZ MARRIAGE REVENGE features Marcello and Shannay, their estrangement, and their three-year-old daughter Nicki. I hope you enjoy their story…

Regards to all readers of romance in this very special Mills & Boon centenary year.

Helen Bianchin

THE MARTINEZ MARRIAGE REVENGE

BY
HELEN BIANCHIN

MILLS & BOON®
Pure reading pleasure

First published in Great Britain 2008
Harlequin Mills & Boon Limited,
Eton House, 18-24 Paradise Road, Richmond, Surrey TW9 1SR

© Helen Bianchin 2008

ISBN: 978 0 263 86408 3

Set in Times Roman 10½ on 12¾ pt
01-0308-44003

Printed and bound in Spain
by Litografia Rosés, S.A., Barcelona

Helen Bianchin was born in New Zealand and travelled to Australia before marrying her Italian-born husband. After three years they moved, returned to New Zealand with their daughter, had two sons, then resettled in Australia. Encouraged by friends to recount anecdotes of her years as a tobacco sharefarmer's wife living in an Italian community, Helen began setting words on paper, and her first novel was published in 1975. An animal lover, she says her terrier and Persian cat regard her study as as much theirs as hers.

CHAPTER ONE

'CAN WE HAVE another turn? Please.'

The noise and colour of the carnival was all around them. Loud music, laughter, childish shrieks in wonderment of the merry-go-round, the Ferris wheel…so many sideshows to capture the attention of a young child.

There were striped tents providing exciting adventure for children, booths selling candyfloss, hot dogs, and stands offering a variety of stuffed toys as prizes for knock-em-down revolving ducks.

Beauty in miniature, Nicki's smile was to die for, her sunny nature a blessing, and Shannay caught her young daughter close in a loving, laughing hug.

Small arms wound round her neck. 'We're having fun, aren't we?'

Shannay felt the familiar pull on her heartstrings for the gift of an unconditional trusting love of a child, in all its innocence.

'One more time,' she agreed, and paid for another ride. 'Then we really need to leave.'

'I know,' Nicki capitulated sunnily. 'You have to go to work.'

'And you need a good night's sleep so you can be bright-eyed at kindergarten tomorrow.'

'So I can grow up and be clever like you.'

The music grew loud, the merry-go-round began to move, and Nicki clutched the reins attached to the brightly painted horse.

OK, so she'd graduated from university with a degree. But not so clever, Shannay mused reflectively, when it came to her personal life.

A broken marriage less than two years after vowing to love and cherish for a lifetime couldn't exactly be viewed as a *plus,* despite mitigating circumstances.

Water under the bridge and no regrets, she assured herself silently as the merry-go-round slowed and drew to an easy halt.

'All done.'

Shannay stepped down and lifted her daughter from the colourful horse.

Beautiful dark eyes sparkled with delicious laughter as she giggled and planted a smacking kiss on her mother's cheek.

Nicki's father's eyes, Shannay reflected, and tamped down the slight tension curling her stomach at the thought of the man she'd married in haste five years ago in another country.

Marcello Martinez, born in France to Spanish parents, raised and educated in Paris, and attended university in Madrid.

Multi-lingual, attractive, sensual, charming…he'd swept her off her feet and into a life far different from her own.

She had told herself she would adjust…and she did, successfully. Or so she'd thought. But not according to his family, who had made it plain she didn't match their élite social status.

An added complication had been the family's favoured choice of a suitable Martinez bride…Estella de Cordova. The stunning raven-haired, dark-eyed socialite possessed impeccable credentials, stellar lineage and obscene wealth.

Something the Martinez family and Estella never permitted Shannay to forget. Or the fact that Marcello and Estella had been lovers…a situation which continued soon after their marriage, if persistent rumour could be believed. Rumour actively fostered by some members of the Martinez family in a bid to diminish Shannay's defences.

Seemingly irrefutable proof of Marcello's infidelity just twenty months after their marriage was the ultimate betrayal, and following an explosive argument Shannay had moved into a hotel and taken the first available flight back to Australia.

Within a matter of weeks she'd obtained a good job in a local pharmacy in suburban Perth, leased an apartment, purchased a car…and become determinedly resolved to dispense Marcello where he belonged.

In her past.

Difficult, when his image had intruded during her daylight hours and haunted her dreams each night.

Impossible, when a persistent stomach upset had necessitated medical examination resulting in the discovery that she was several weeks pregnant.

It seemed incredibly ironic, given how desperately she'd hoped to gift Marcello a child, that confirmation of conception should occur when the marriage was already shattered, with legal dissolution a distinct probability.

The decision not to inform Marcello about his impending fatherhood continued through pregnancy, initially due to fear of a possible miscarriage, and afterwards Shannay had become so fiercely maternal, enlightening him just hadn't been a considered option.

As a precaution, she'd covered her tracks successfully, resorting to her late mother's maiden name and ensuring any mail directed to her arrived via a circuitous route.

Now, almost four years after fleeing Madrid, life was good.

Ordered, she elaborated mentally. She owned an apartment in a modern, upscale building in suburban Applecross, and she worked the five-to-midnight shift as a registered pharmacist not far from her home. Ideal, for it enabled her to spend the days with Nicki, and for her to also pay Anna, a kindly widow in a neighbouring apartment, to sit with Nicki each evening.

'Can I take some candyfloss home to share with Anna?' Nicki's earnest expression was pleadingly angelic.

'I promise I'll brush my teeth afterwards.'

Shannay opened her mouth to offer the diced organic cantaloupe melon she'd stored in a small container as a snack in her backpack, only to change her mind. 'OK.' And refrained from adding any caution. What was a visit to a carnival without sampling candyfloss?

Nicki's face lit up with delighted pleasure. 'Love you, Mummy. You're the best.'

Shannay hugged her daughter close. 'Love you, too, imp.' She laughed and bent low to kiss Nicki's cheek. 'Candyfloss it is. Then we hit the road for home.'

She lifted her head…and froze with shock as her gaze locked on two people she'd thought never to see again. *Hoping* no member of the Martinez family would ever cross her path.

What were the chances, when they resided on opposite sides of the world?

And why *here,* at a carnival camped on council park grounds in suburban Perth?

Did a heart stop beating? She was willing to swear hers did before it accelerated again into a maddened tattoo.

Recognition was clearly apparent, and with it the indisputable knowledge there could be no escape.

'Shannay.' There was an imperceptible pause as Sandro Martinez marshalled his expression into polite civility.

Her chin lifted as she held Marcello's younger brother's intently speculative gaze as it shifted to Nicki and lingered over-long, before returning to fix on her own.

'Sandro.' Cool, *polite*...she could do both. 'Luisa,' she acknowledged the young woman at his side.

She had to get away. *Now*.

'Mummy?'

No. From the mouth of an innocent child came the one word which removed any element of doubt as to whom Nicki belonged.

Shannay saw Sandro's mouth tighten into an uncompromising line. 'Your daughter?'

Before she could offer a word, Nicki offered a solemnly voiced— 'My name is Nicki, and I'm three.'

Oh, sweetheart, she almost groaned aloud. Do you have any idea what you've just done?

The silent accusation in Sandro's dark eyes alarmed her, and she had no doubt had she been alone he'd have delivered a blistering no-holds-barred denunciation.

The Martinez familial ties were so strong Shannay knew there wasn't a snowflake's chance in hell that Sandro would remain silent.

She barely resisted the urge to gather Nicki into her arms and run, test the speed limit to the place she called home...and pack. Take a flight to the east coast and lose herself in another city.

'If you'll excuse me?' she managed coolly. 'We're already late.'

Shannay tightened her hold on Nicki's hand, then she turned away and forced herself to walk with controlled ease toward the exit, her back straight and her head held high.

Pride. She had it in spades. And she refused to take a backward glance as they were swallowed up by the crowd.

Could a stomach twist into a painful ball? It felt as if hers did, and the blood in her veins turned to ice as she clipped Nicki into her booster seat in the rear of her compact sedan.

'We forgot the candyfloss.'

Oh, hell. 'We'll get some on the way home.' The supermarket sold it in packets. She fired the engine and put the car in drive.

'It won't be the same,' Nicki offered without rancour.

No, it wouldn't. Oh, damn. *Dammit,* she cursed beneath her breath. If they hadn't taken another turn on the merry-go-round…

But they had done. And it was too late for recriminations now.

Shannay headed towards her suburban apartment and went into automatic pilot as she bathed and changed Nicki, readied herself for work, then she handed her daughter into Anna's care and drove to the pharmacy.

Somehow she managed to get through the evening, dispensing medications and offering advice to customers who sought it.

Concern, fear, dread…the palpable mix heightened her tension to almost breaking point, and by closing time she'd developed a doozy of a headache.

It was a relief to reach the sanctuary of her apartment, thank Anna, check on Nicki, then undress and slip into bed.

But not to sleep.

Estimating her estranged husband's reaction on discovering she had a child…*his* child, didn't bear thinking about.

Could she insist *he* wasn't Nicki's father?

A hollow laugh rose and died in her throat.

All Marcello had to do was insist on a DNA paternity test to shoot that one out of the water.

And afterwards?

A slight shiver shook her slender form.

Marcello was a ruthless strategist, possessed of sufficient power and wealth to dispense with anyone or anything that might stand in his path.

Shannay was the exception.

She'd make sure of it.

No one would be permitted to come between her and Nicki.

No one.

A resolve which remained uppermost when she woke next morning, and strengthened with each passing hour. Together with an increasing degree of nervous tension.

It wasn't a matter of *if,* but *when* Marcello would make contact. Either in person, or via legal representation.

Marcello Martinez might not care about *her.* But a child, indisputably *his* child, would be another matter entirely.

Given Sandro could pinpoint her location, just how difficult would it be for someone of Marcello's calibre to discover where she lived and worked?

A piece of cake, a silent voice assured in taunting response.

Knowledge which didn't sit well. She barely ate and every waking hour was spent attempting to predict any possible scenario Marcello might choose to present.

The necessity to ensure Anna take every precaution while Nicki was in her care resulted in only one query.

'Are you in trouble with the law?'

Oh, dear God. 'No…*no,* of course not,' Shannay reiterated.

'That's all I need to know.'

An apparently single mother and child… How difficult was it to do the maths and reach the conclusion of a looming custody battle?

'Thanks,' she expressed with genuine gratitude.

How long would it take Marcello to plan his strategy and put it into action?

A few days? A week?

Meantime, she needed to consult a lawyer to spell out her legal rights in fine detail. She was aware of the basics, and sufficiently astute to realise what appeared logical and rational didn't always hold true.

She also intended to file for divorce.

Given she could prove a separation of more than the legal requirement, it should only be a matter of time before she gained a dissolution of the marriage.

Whereupon the only issue that could arise would be *custody*.

An icy chill invaded her body and settled in her bones.

Marcello couldn't enforce custody of Nicki…surely?

What rights would he possibly have?

Shannay wrapped her arms tightly over her midriff, and barely prevented her body from shaking with very real fear.

Her soon-to-be ex-husband possessed the wealth and the power to surmount any objective he set out to achieve.

A silent scream echoed inside her brain.

If he decided he wanted Nicki, then he'd move heaven and earth to get her.

Over my dead body, Shannay resolved.

CHAPTER TWO

MARCELLO MARTINEZ moved through the international-terminal lounge with Carlo, his personal assistant and trusted bodyguard, at his side, seemingly unaware of the speculative interest in his tall, broad frame.

The Martinez legacy had gifted him the compelling well-defined features of his forefathers, arresting, wide-set dark, almost black eyes which projected the hardness of a man well-versed in the frailty of human nature.

There was an aura of power and intense masculinity apparent, together with a dangerous ruthlessness that boded ill for any adversary.

He was linked to Spanish nobility, with a personal wealth that placed him high on a list of the European rich.

And it showed…as he meant it to do, from the Armani tailoring, hand-stitched Italian shoes, to the fine Rolex at his wrist.

The long flight had done little to ease the anger simmering beneath his control. The luxuriously fitted Gulf Stream privately owned jet offered every comfort, geared with the latest technology enabling him to have an essential office in the sky.

* * *

Although he'd worked, studying print-outs, graphs and data, checked his BlackBerry and kept in touch with Sandro…he hadn't been able to switch off and sleep.

Something he usually achieved at will, given the comfortable bed situated with its own *en suite* at the rear of the jet.

Instead he was plagued by a young woman's image, startlingly vivid and recently taken via camera phone.

Shannay Martinez…née Robbins.

And his daughter.

The *before* and *after* shots.

The first serene, happy and loving. Mother and child, laughing.

In the second image, the child's expression remained the same. His estranged wife's features, however, mirrored shock and something else…

The innate knowledge *life* as she'd known it since leaving Spain was about to change?

Without doubt.

A muscle bunched at the edge of his jaw as he exited the terminal's automatic glass doors and stepped into a limousine waiting at the kerb.

The chauffeur stowed his bags in the boot and moved up front to slide in behind the wheel.

Marcello barely noticed the passing scene beyond the tinted windows as the limousine left the airport and began picking up speed *en route* to the city.

A child.

Anger, barely held in control since Sandro's enlightening phone call, rose to the surface.

How *dared* Shannay keep him in ignorance of the child's existence?

His initial reaction had been to instruct his pilot to ready the Gulf Stream jet for an immediate flight to Australia.

Instead, he'd delegated with icy calm, consulted his legal team and planned his strategy.

Tomorrow he intended to bring it into play.

Marcello's suite in the inner-city hotel offered first-class luxury, and with practised ease he shrugged off his jacket, discarded his tie, organised his unpacking and settled down to peruse the report handed to him on check-in.

The private-investigation resource he'd utilised had done a good job. The document revealed a detailed listing of Shannay's movements over the past few days, her address, unlisted telephone number, the make, model and registration of her car, place of work, Nicki's kindergarten facility.

Details which filled in some of the blanks, and revealed she hadn't touched so much as a cent of the money he'd initially deposited into a bank account bearing her name. Or the amount he'd contributed each month since.

He wanted to *shake* her, and would have if she'd been within reach.

What was she trying to prove?

Something he already knew.

His family connections, his wealth and social status had never impressed her.

She'd fallen into his life, literally, he mused, recalling the moment the fine heel of one of her stilettos had become caught in a metal grating and had pitched her against him on a busy city street in the heart of Madrid.

He'd been unprepared for the instantaneous physical chemistry…and an instinctive need to lengthen contact with her.

They'd shared coffee in a nearby upmarket café, exchanged cellphone numbers…and the rest was history. Marcello closed the report and crossed to the wide expanse of double-glazed glass offering a brilliant view of the Swan river.

The sky provided an azure backdrop to tall city buildings, selected greenery…a colourful panoramic pictorial, he noted absently, reminding him of a similar visit a few brief years ago when his ring on Shannay's finger had claimed her as his wife.

A time when they couldn't get enough of each other, and had rarely spent a moment apart.

Marcello felt his body tighten at the memory of all that they'd shared. Her uninhibited enthusiasm, her laughter, her passion.

His own libidinous response and loss of control.

Something he'd never experienced with another woman to the same degree.

Or in any other area of his life.

He held a reputation in the business arena for icy calm in any volatile situation. A trait which earned him the respect of his contemporaries.

With a slow roll of his shoulders he turned away from the plate-glass window and checked his watch.

It had been a long flight, crossing countries, entering another time zone and the need to adjust to it.

Stroking several punishing laps in the hotel pool, followed by a session in the gym, would help iron out any kinks and ease the tension.

With that in mind he keyed a text message to Carlo, then he shed his clothes, donned swimming trunks, shrugged on a complimentary robe, caught up a towel, essentials, and took the lift to the appropriate floor.

An hour and a half later, showered and dressed in a formal business suit, he walked out into the late-afternoon sunshine, stepped into his chauffeured limousine and instructed the driver to deliver him to a mid-town address.

The highly qualified Perth-based lawyer engaged by Marcello's legal team to represent his Australian interests confirmed certain legalities, offered assurances and advice on procedure, and the consultation concluded at the close of the business day.

On his return to the hotel he shed his jacket and tie, ordered a meal from Room Service, connected his laptop to the internet and engaged a link to his Madrid office.

Shannay crouched down to Nicki's eye level and caught her close, whispered "Love you", and heard her daughter's "Love you back", then she rose fluidly to her full height and smoothed a gentle hand over Nicki's head.

'Have a fun day.'

Kindergarten was carefully structured, mostly fun and, importantly, Nicki loved spending time with the other children as they moved from play-dough to finger-painting, played games and listened to stories read by one of the carers.

'You, too.'

Nicki happily moved to her place on the mat and Shannay hid a soft smile as Nicki engaged in animated chatter with one of her friends.

Time to leave, get into her car and head home. There were phone calls and household chores to complete before returning to collect her daughter.

A short while later she exchanged fitted jeans and tailored shirt for shorts and a cropped top, then she set to work.

Dusting, mopping and polishing helped Shannay expend some nervous energy, and she wielded the vacuum cleaner with zealous speed.

Another five minutes and she'd be done, then she'd hit the

shower, dress, make the few calls and head off to Nicki's kindergarten facility.

The ring of the in-house phone was barely audible above the sound of the vacuum cleaner, and she shut it down, then she crossed the room and tamped down a strange prickling sense of foreboding…which was crazy.

For several days she'd been on tenterhooks waiting for Marcello to make his move, agonising when it would happen and what it might entail.

Oh, for heaven's sake, she railed in silent self-castigation. It could be anyone buzzing her apartment…so take a deep breath and go check the security-video screen.

The tight security features employed here were some of the main reasons she'd purchased the apartment.

Protection and safety were an issue in any large city, and she rested more easily knowing she'd taken every available precaution.

The insistent ring of the buzzer impelled her to cross the room…and her breath hitched painfully in her throat the moment she recognised the male figure revealed on-screen.

Marcello Martinez…in person.

His monochrome image did little to detract from his forceful features…the strong facial bone structure, piercing gaze and well-shaped mouth.

Shannay felt her stomach muscles clench in unbidden reaction, for it took only one look at him for all the memories to flood back.

The good ones where his care and passion ignited something wild deep within her soul…and the not-so good when the arguments began to escalate into varying degrees of anger.

Pick up, why don't you?

Delaying the inevitable wouldn't achieve a thing.

Her fingers shook a little as she caught hold of the receiver, intoned a brief acknowledgment and saw his features harden.

'Buzz me in, Shannay. We need to talk.'

She bit back an angry retort. 'I have nothing to say to you.'

For a moment his gaze became faintly hooded, and his voice assumed a dangerous silkiness. 'I intend to see my daughter.'

'You have no proof she's yours,' she was goaded into stating.

His dark eyes seemed to pierce her own via the video link. 'You want to do this the hard way?'

'We lost the art of polite dialogue a long time ago.'

Marcello's expression hardened, and she had the uncanny sensation he could *see* her...which was, of course, impossible.

Yet that fact did little to aid reassurance, or prevent the shivery finger of fear feathering the length of her spine.

It was easy to close down the video screen. Not so easy to cast him out of her mind, and his forceful image refused to subside despite every effort she made to conquer it as she quickly showered, pulled on black dress jeans, added a singlet top, some *faux* bling, swept her hair into a casual twist and applied minimum make-up.

Then she caught up her bag, collected keys, locked the apartment and took the lift down to the basement car park. Nervous tension rose up a notch as the doors slid open, and she stepped out and began walking towards her sedan...only to falter fractionally as she caught sight of a tall male figure leaning against the passenger door.

CHAPTER THREE

MARCELLO.

With one hand resting in his trouser pocket, the casual stance portrayed studied indolence…a look she knew to be misleading, for it bore the stamp of a predator awaiting the opportunity to strike.

For a wild second she considered turning back towards the lift. Except she refused to give him the satisfaction.

Besides, it was paramount she collect Nicki from kindergarten.

He wanted a confrontation? She'd darned well give him one!

Shannay lifted her chin and fixed him with a determined look…which presumably had little or no effect, for his position remained unchanged as she drew close.

Her shoulders lifted, she straightened her back and she fearlessly met his dark, almost black eyes.

OK, so she'd start out being civil. 'Marcello.'

'Shannay.'

The timbre of his faintly accented voice curled round her nerve-ends and tugged…much to her dismay. She didn't want to be affected by him, nor did she want any reminder of what they'd shared.

Which was a travesty, given the fact that they had Nicki's existence as living proof!

'This is a private car park.'

One eyebrow slanted in open mockery. 'Next, you'll ask how I accessed entry.'

'I don't have time for idle conversation.' She made a point of checking her watch.

'Then we should get straight to the point.'

His drawled response rankled, and she determinedly ignored the icy chill scudding the length of her spine.

'Which is?' As if she didn't know!

Eyes as dark as sin became hard and implacable. 'My daughter.'

His raking appraisal was unsettling, and she made a concentrated effort to strengthen her resolve.

'The father is not listed on her birth certificate.'

A protective choice at the time, and, she had to admit, motivated by an act of defiance.

'I've accessed hospital records,' Marcello enlightened with deadly softness. 'Nicki was born full-term. Which narrows down the time of her conception to around six weeks before you left Madrid.'

She knew what was coming, and she closed her eyes as if the action would prevent the damning words he would inevitably relay.

'I've authorised a DNA paternity test through a private biolab.' He waited a beat. 'They have my sample, and require one from Nicki, preferably within the next twenty-four hours.' A muscle bunched at his jaw. 'I have the requisite paperwork for you to sign.'

She wanted to hit him...*hard,* preferably where it would hurt the most.

'No.' Her voice was terse as she battled with her anger, and his eyes hardened.

'You refuse permission?'

'Yes, damn you!'

'Then I file for custody, and it gets ugly.'

The chilling finality in his voice succeeded in sending a wave of fear washing through Shannay's body.

He could command the finest legal brains in the country to present a case in his favour.

No surprise there. It was a measure of the man to ensure every detail was in place before he struck.

'You bastard.'

One eyebrow lifted in a gesture of deliberate cynicism. 'No descriptive adjectives, Shannay?'

'Too many,' she owned grimly, hating him more than she'd hated anyone in her life.

'Your call. You have twenty-four hours to provide me with your decision.'

Her eyes sparked dark fire. 'Go to hell, Marcello.'

He extracted a card and held it out to her. 'My cellphone number. Call me.'

'Not in this millennium.'

The atmosphere between them became so highly charged it threatened to ignite.

Marcello's eyebrow slanted in visible mockery. 'Perhaps you should reconsider, given I'm aware of your address, Nicki's kindergarten, the park you both frequently visit.' His expression didn't change. 'Shall I go on?'

Consternation filled her at the thought he might appear un-announced at any of those places…the effect he would have without suitable introduction and explanation.

'You'd do that?' Shannay demanded, stricken at the mere thought. 'Frighten, even *abduct* her?'

'Mierda.' His voice was husky with anger, his features a hard mask. 'What kind of man do you think I am?'

She thought she knew *once*. Now too much was at stake for her to even hazard a guess.

'I intend to meet her, spend some time in her company.' Chilling bleak eyes trapped hers. 'Accept it's going to happen, Shannay.' His pause was imperceptible. 'One way or another.'

He was giving her a choice, that much was clear…The easy way, or via a legal minefield.

She momentarily closed her eyes against the sight of him, hating the position he was placing her in.

It was on the tip of her tongue to tell him to go to hell, and be damned.

For herself, she didn't care. But she was fiercely protective of her daughter, and she'd tread over hot coals before she'd willingly expose Nicki to anything that would upset or destroy her trust.

'You're a ruthless son-of-a-bitch.' Her voice was filled with bitterness, and he merely inclined his head.

'So what else is new?'

'Nicki is *mine. I* chose to carry her, give birth to her.' Her eyes blazed with pent-up emotion. 'I was the one to nurture and love her.'

A muscle tensed close to his jaw. 'You denied me the opportunity to be there.'

'We were *through!*'

'You opted out.'

The correction hurt. 'Instead of staying to fight for you?' She offered a dismissive gesture and her voice became husky.

'*Please.* I hit my head against a figurative brick wall at every turn. In the end, your mistress and your family won.'

His eyes narrowed. 'You were my wife.'

The '*were*' did it, and her chin tilted as she flung him a look of blazing defiance. 'Fat lot of difference that made.'

'I gave my vow of fidelity,' he reminded with pitiless disregard, watching the conflicting emotions chase fleetingly across her expressive features.

Shannay didn't want to think of their wedding day, or the days and weeks that had followed when everything in their world had seemed perfect. Until reality intervened, insidiously at first, until she was forced to recognise the manipulative calculation of planned destruction.

'Empty words, Marcello?'

'This is old ground, is it not? Now there is a more pressing matter to be resolved.'

Nicki.

Shannay felt pain shaft through her body, and her features became strained.

'Where would you prefer to meet?' he pursued hardily. 'The kindergarten or your apartment?'

Dear heaven, *no.* 'Not the kindergarten.' Her mind scrambled for a compromise.

Nor the apartment. She couldn't bear to have him invade her sanctuary, her space, where he'd assume control and she'd have to sacrifice her own in Nicki's presence…or risk a situation which would alarm her daughter.

Lunch. She could do lunch. Somewhere child-friendly that Nicki was familiar with, and they'd keep it short and sweet…the shorter the better.

She named a venue and stated a time. 'Tomorrow,' she added, and saw his mouth tighten.

'Today.'

'No,' she said firmly. She needed to assume some form of control in the situation.

His gaze seemed to bore into hers. '*Today*, Shannay. Twelve-thirty.' He paused imperceptibly, and his voice became deadly quiet. 'Be there.'

Today. Tomorrow. What was the difference? How would twenty-four hours change anything?

Marcello was *here*. And now she had no recourse but to deal with the situation.

'If—*if*,' she stressed, 'I agree, there would need to be conditions.'

'Such as?'

A pulse beat fast at the base of her throat, a visible sign of her inner turmoil.

Marcello regarded her steadily, noting the darkness of her eyes, the faint shadows beneath, and her pale features.

It would seem she hadn't slept any better than he, and there was a certain satisfaction to be had in that.

'As far as Nicki is concerned, you're just—' she hesitated, aware *friend* wasn't the word she wanted to use '—someone I know.'

Marcello felt like shaking her, and barely controlled the need. 'And when the paternity test reveals otherwise?'

Shannay's features whitened dramatically. She really didn't want to go there…at least, not until she had to. She checked her watch, and felt her stomach curl with apprehension. 'I have to leave now, Marcello.' Even if the traffic lights were in her favour, she was going to be late picking Nicki up.

Marcello straightened and extracted a set of keys. 'I'll follow at a discreet distance.'

Her eyes flared. 'Because you don't trust me?'

'It's a more simple process than consulting a map.'

Without a further word he crossed to a sleek sedan and slid in behind the wheel.

The sound of the car's engine igniting galvanised Shannay into action, and she quickly copied him as she sent her car onto street level.

Dammit, she silently fumed. Who did he think he was?

A man who made his own rules and expected others to abide by them, she conceded grimly.

Nicki was waiting with a carer when Shannay entered the kindergarten, and she offered an apology, gave Nicki a reassuring hug, then she elicited a brief update on the morning before catching hold of her daughter's hand as she led the way out towards the car.

She deliberately didn't glance towards the street to check if Marcello's sedan was parked in the vicinity.

'We're going out for a while.' She kept her voice light, bright, as she attempted to still the nervous tension spiralling through her body.

'To the park?' Nicki queried hopefully. 'Can we feed the ducks?'

Shannay fervently wished such a simple pleasure as eating a packed lunch in the park formed part of the day as she lifted Nicki into her booster seat and secured the safety fastenings.

She leaned in close and dropped a light kiss on her daughter's nose. 'After lunch, on the way home,' she promised, aware there was no better time than now to impart whom they were meeting and why.

'A friend of mine is visiting from Spain, and he's invited us to share lunch with him.' She smoothed a hand over Nicki's hair and summoned a smile. 'Won't that be fun?'

Oh, sure, and little pink pigs should sprout wings and fly!

How could she state *this man is your father?*

Worse, voice her deepest fear…

Traffic was light, and she fought the temptation to take the route back to her apartment. Only the knowledge Marcello would seek her out and make the situation incredibly more difficult than it already was ensured she drove to the restaurant.

Taking a circuitous route was a minor act of defiance.

Did he know? Possibly. Although he gave no indication as she effected an introduction…and watched dry-mouthed as Marcello hunkered down to Nicki's eye level.

Shannay stood tense and incredibly protective…anxious to the point of paranoia over her daughter's reaction to the man who posed such a potent threat to their existence.

Quite what she expected, she wasn't sure.

She was intently aware of Marcello, but it was Nicki who held her undivided attention.

Outgoing, polite and friendly, Nicki regarded Marcello with wide-eyed unblinking solemnity. Weighing him up with the innocence of youth, reserving judgement until instinct dismissed an initial wariness and a smile curved her mouth.

'Hello. I'm Nicki.' Unbidden, a small hand extended in formal greeting, and with great care Marcello enfolded it within his own.

Hearts didn't melt, stomachs didn't really perform somersaults…but it sure felt like hers did both as conflicting emotions took hold with unsettling reality.

Father and child.

There was a part of her that wanted to encapsulate the moment for safe-keeping…for Nicki, she assured herself silently.

The venue proved eminently suitable, the food pleasantly presented and palatable. Not, Shannay mused, what her estranged husband was used to, but perfect for a young child.

It was difficult to summon light laughter and appear relaxed and at ease, when inside she'd have given anything for Marcello to be anywhere but *here*.

Maintaining the pretence of friendship proved to be a strain, and she battled emotional turmoil at the developing rapport between father and child.

Why shouldn't Nicki be entranced by the man her mother had introduced as *friend?* The mere appellation sanctioned approval, and heaven knew Marcello possessed innate charm when he chose to employ it.

And he did, with an ease Shannay could only reluctantly admire, whilst silently hating him for capturing her daughter's innocent heart.

'We're going to stop and feed the ducks on the way home,' Nicki announced as Marcello took care of the bill.

Shannay's offer to contribute her share merely incurred a telling glance, and she accepted his refusal with grace.

'That sounds like fun,' Marcello said gently, and Nicki laughed with delight.

'You can come, too, if you like.'

Please don't, Shannay silently begged. Lunch was enough. If she had to spend any more time in his company, it would be way too much.

He pocketed his wallet and gave Nicki his whole attention. 'I have another appointment this afternoon. But I'd like to watch you feed the ducks another day.'

'Tomorrow?'

Marcello spared Shannay a glance. 'If it's all right with your mother?'

Thanks for putting me in such an invidious position! A refusal would be petty, and disappoint her daughter. Besides, she was damned if she'd give Marcello the satisfaction.

She summoned a smiling assent. 'Tomorrow's fine.' A short sojourn, then she'd plead the need to take Nicki home.

'Perhaps we could share a picnic lunch.'

Nicki clapped her hands together in delight. 'I love picnics.'

If looks could kill, Marcello mused, he'd be dead. Although he had to concede Shannay covered it well. As to his daughter—*his,* without a shred of doubt—he was hard-pressed not to scoop her into his arms.

He'd expected to feel a connection, even a degree of affection. But this deep encompassing bond surprised him completely.

Marcello copied Shannay's actions and rose to his feet. His gaze skimmed her averted features and settled on bright, innocent brown eyes. 'We have a date.'

'A date,' Nicki repeated as she reached for her mother's hand, unaware of the tension simmering between the two adults.

OK, so you're in the minority here, Shannay conceded silently, and wanted to cry *foul.* It wasn't fair of Marcello to manipulate a child.

But then Marcello was ruthless when in pursuit of what he wanted…and he wanted Nicki.

They exited the restaurant and crossed to the adjoining car park.

'Thank you for lunch.' She could do polite, as an essential example in good manners. She caught the faint gleam apparent in his eyes, and determinedly ignored it.

He extracted a slim envelope from his suit-jacket pocket and handed it to her. 'The permission form. Sign and return it to me tomorrow.'

The DNA paternity test.

She could stall him.

How long? A few days…a week?

If she refused and he was forced to travel the legal route…

'Don't,' Marcello cautioned quietly.

How was it possible for one small word to hold such a wealth of meaning?

Supremely conscious of Nicki's interested attention, she slid the envelope into her bag, proffered a superficial smile and led Nicki to the car, aware of his presence as she settled her daughter safely in the rear seat.

'See you tomorrow,' Nicki bade as Marcello opened the door to allow Shannay to slide in behind the wheel.

His mouth parted in a warm smile that skimmed lightly over Nicki's trusting features and settled briefly on her own.

For a few interminable seconds she was caught in the thrall of remembered chemistry. Jolted by the sensuality that coursed through her veins, unbidden, electric…and definitely unwanted.

It had been *there,* simmering beneath the surface from the moment she'd heard his voice. Seeing him, sharing his company only made it worse.

For she was forced to recall memories, evocative, spell-binding in their intensity.

Even now, her body seemed to recognise his, and she attempted to control the curl of sensual emotion stirring deep within.

She didn't want to remember the all-consuming passion, the feel of his hands, his mouth…how she'd lost herself so completely in him.

Go, a silent voice urged.

Ignite the engine and leave.

Now.

Somehow she managed to get through the remainder of the day, and she bore Nicki's excited chatter about "Mummy's friend" and the proposed picnic as she bathed and fed Nicki, then readied herself for work.

'I have lots to tell Anna.'

Shannay leant down and kissed her daughter's cheek as the doorbell rang. 'Be good, hmm?'

'Always,' Nicki responded solemnly.

A light chuckle emerged from her throat. 'Imp.'

'A nice imp.'

Shannay gathered her in for a hug, then smoothed a hand over dark curls. 'Extra-specially nice,' she agreed, and crossed to let Anna into the apartment.

CHAPTER FOUR

MARCELLO'S IMAGE haunted Shannay's subconscious and provided scattered dreams which seemed to reach nightmarish proportion throughout the night.

Consequently she woke to the insistent sound of the alarm clock feeling as if she hadn't slept at all.

Not good.

She had a responsible job, she worked nights, and right now she'd give anything to bury her head in the pillow, snatch an hour's dreamless sleep, and face an untroubled day.

Not possible.

'Are you awake, Mummy?'

Bright eyes, tousled hair, a smile to die for…the light of her life.

Shannay reached for her daughter, gathered her close and pressed a light kiss to Nicki's forehead.

'Morning, sweetheart.'

'We're going to the park for a picnic today.'

'Uh-huh.' She playfully tickled Nicki's ribs and the action brought forth a series of giggles. 'Time to rise and shine, dress, have breakfast and—'

'Be on the road by nine,' Nicki completed a familiar mantra as she slid from the bed.

The picnic, the ducks, Marcello.

Not necessarily in that order, although combined they were the sole topic of Nicki's conversation that morning.

Shannay gritted her teeth as she headed home after delivering her daughter to kindergarten.

If she heard his name mentioned again, she'd…do or say something regrettable!

One hour in his company, and he held Nicki in his thrall.

It was so not fair. And so typical of the man's effect on the female species.

Traffic lights up ahead changed and she eased the car to a halt.

Figuratively speaking she was between a rock and a hard place. Signing or not signing the DNA paternity form only presented a relatively minor issue compared to the big picture.

The demons of the night returned tenfold, and the sudden strident sound of a car horn thrust her back into the present.

The insistent burr of her cellphone within minutes of clearing the intersection resulted in a juggling action as she changed lanes and pulled over to take the call.

'Shannay.'

The familiar faintly accented male voice upped her nervous tension by several notches, and it took effort to summon a cool acknowledgement.

'What do you want?'

'We need to talk. There's a café not far from your apartment. Meet me there in ten minutes.'

'I have things to do, Marcello.'

'This morning,' Marcello elaborated, 'in Nicki's presence, or during your evening work hours, we will talk.'

'You can't—' The words spilled, only to stop mid-sentence. He had no scruples whatsoever when it came to achieving his objective.

'Choose.'

She could feel the anger surging through her body, and at that moment she truly hated him. 'There is no choice.'

'I'll order a latte for you.'

Damn him to hell. It was on the tip of her tongue to tell him exactly what he could do with the latte, except in some instances silence was golden, and she simply cut the connection.

Shannay reached her apartment block and eased the car down into the underground car park, locked it, then took the lift to ground level and walked out into the morning sunshine.

The café was close by, upmarket with outdoor tables and boutique sun umbrellas. A meeting place where friends assembled over designer coffee and sumptuous food to talk business, chat and watch the world go by.

There, seated outdoors, was Marcello.

Absent was the designer business suit, for today he'd chosen casual dark chinos and a white shirt unbuttoned at the neck.

It lent him a relaxed façade…one she knew to be misleading. Despite appearances to the contrary, Marcello rarely lowered his guard. It was what he'd become, who he was…and it showed.

There was something exigent that wrought a second look, a curiosity, sometimes fleeting, to check the level of power he emanated. A hint of the primitive, which unleashed could cause untold sensual havoc to a woman's equilibrium.

A quality other men admired and coveted, but few possessed.

Marcello glanced up as she approached, and she felt the full impact of those dark eyes as they seared her own, witnessing for one moment the naked vulnerability apparent before she successfully masked it.

He signalled the waitress as Shannay slid into a seat opposite him.

Make-up free, except for a touch of gloss to her mouth, her hair caught together with a decorative clip, and dressed in jeans and a singlet top she looked scarcely more than a teenager.

Except looks could be deceptive, he mused, all too aware of the latent passion that lurked beneath that cool façade.

He remembered too well the sensual delight of her body, the persuasive touch and her eagerness to share…everything.

Heat unfurled and ran hot as he felt his own unbidden response, the need to render her willing and wanton. *His*, as she had been…and would be again.

No other woman came close, and he'd wanted what he once had.

Worse, he wanted her to pay for attempting to deny him any knowledge of his daughter.

'Shannay.'

The waitress delivered her latte, and she selected two sugar tubes, broke them open and stirred in the contents.

Shannay took a deliberate sip of the frothy, milky liquid, then she carefully replaced the glass onto its saucer and met Marcello's studied gaze.

'Let's get this over with, shall we?' she suggested coolly.

'Put our cards on the table, so to speak?' Marcello drawled.

He was a superb strategist who played the game according to his own rules…and inevitably saved the sting for a *coup de grâce*.

Estimating precisely what that would encompass had kept her awake many nights and had haunted her dreams for a long time.

'Yes.' Delay wouldn't achieve a thing, and wasn't discovering the enemy's game-plan half the battle?

'The initial step is establishing legal evidence of my paternity.'

'Something I won't consent to without being fully aware of your intentions.' Her voice was even, polite. 'Immediate and long term.'

His eyes narrowed fractionally. 'Whatever is decided will be primarily in Nicki's best interests,' he assured with hateful ease.

'How can that be so?' Shannay demanded, glaring at him. 'Establishing custody rights will provide a total disruption to her life. Schooling, friends, family. Any hope of *stability*.' She could feel herself winding up. 'I'm her mother, *dammit*.'

He looked at her for what seemed an age, noting the fine edge of her anger, the restrained need to fight him…regardless of common-sense.

'Nicki hasn't displayed any curiosity about the absence of a father in her life?'

She ignored the silkiness in his voice, the latent anger held in tight control, and her eyes sharpened beneath the dark inflexibility evident in his.

'Inevitably, soon after she began attending kindergarten,' she revealed.

'And?'

Her gaze didn't waver. 'I told her the very basic truth.'

An eyebrow lifted. 'Enlighten me.'

'I left her father before she was born.' She lifted a hand and smoothed it over her hair in an unconscious gesture. 'A number of children have single parents nowadays.'

Marcello leaned back in his chair and regarded her thoughtfully. 'Except you're still married, Shannay. To me.'

'Not for much longer.'

His smile was a faint facsimile. 'In four years you have only considered filing for divorce now?'

'I'm not part of one of your business deals, Marcello. So quit playing psychological games.' Shannay buttoned down her frustrated anger. 'Spell out exactly what you intend.'

For a moment she imagined she glimpsed a fleeting shadow in the depth of his eyes, only to dismiss it.

'With Nicki?'

'Of course, with Nicki!'

'Initially, I want to gift a sick elderly man the opportunity to meet his only great-grandchild.'

It wasn't the answer she expected, nor was the mixture of emotions that tore at her heart. 'Ramon is ill?'

The one person who had attempted to smooth over the family discord at Marcello's choice of a wife. Someone who saw more than anyone intended, and became her ally. 'How ill?'

'The medical professionals predict he has only a matter of months. Maybe less.'

The implications assumed vivid reality. Achieving his objective would involve taking Nicki to Spain.

Pain escalated as it raced through her body, consuming her mind with turmoil. 'I won't allow you to take her overseas.' Rationality went out the window. 'She doesn't have a passport. Hell, she doesn't even *know* you!'

What if he didn't bring Nicki back?

What if Nicki became distressed, distraught…?

'Naturally, you would accompany her.'

Revisit a place where she had spent the worst twenty months of her life?

Mix with a family who hid their disapproval of Marcello's choice of a wife beneath a thin veneer of politeness? A former lover, touted not to be so *former,* who delighted in causing mischief and mayhem?

'You have to be kidding!'

'A few weeks,' Marcello elaborated. 'That's all.'

Shannay closed her eyes, then opened them again. 'No.'

'I gave Ramon my word.'

Something which only made the situation worse. 'Ramon knows about Nicki?'

'My grandfather was—' he paused fractionally '—inadvertently appraised of Nicki's existence.'

It wasn't difficult to do the maths. 'Penè.' Marcello's widowed aunt, a disgruntled woman who took delight in running interference.

She had no difficulty envisaging Sandro informing Marcello of his chance encounter a week ago, or the manner in which Penè came to hear of it.

Happy families. *Not.*

There was more. Ramon's illness was only a part of it.

Her eyes narrowed. 'And?'

One eyebrow slanted in silent query.

She took a deliberate sip of coffee, then another, before replacing the glass onto its saucer as she speared him with a direct look.

'I don't doubt the validity of your request. But don't attempt to use it as a smokescreen.' Did he think she was a naive fool?

'Why would I do that?'

Shannay had positioned the figurative nail, now she chose to hammer it home. 'To gain my sympathy, and dilute the major issue here.' She waited a beat. 'Your plans to gain custody.' Her expression hardened a little. 'Or is that not to form part of this *discussion,* and you'll instruct your legal representative to inform mine of your intention?'

She was fearless when it came to protecting her child. He admired her strength and determination…and pondered if she was fully aware it was no match for his.

'It will take time to work out a mutually amicable custody agreement,' Marcello offered with deceptive indolence. 'We need to consult and compare our individual schedules, and above all, ensure the arrangements we propose suit Nicki's best interests. Her emotional welfare is the priority, is it not?'

Defensive assurance rose to the fore. 'My daughter's emotional status is just fine as it is.'

'But circumstances have changed,' he posed with deliberate calm. 'Nicki is no longer the child of one parent. She has two. The legal system is purported to be fair. If we're unable to reach an amicable agreement, a court judge will review our respective cases and award custody.' He paused deliberately, his gaze intent on her expressive features. 'Given the facts, do you doubt any judge will deny me reasonable access to my daughter?'

No, she conceded the hollow knowledge. But she was confident she could insist such access be confined within Australia.

'Why do I get the feeling there's an underlying reason behind all this?' she demanded with increasing vexation.

'One you obviously haven't considered,' Marcello ventured, then elaborated with faint emphasis. 'Nicki's rightful inheritance as a legitimate member of the Martinez dynasty.'

Her chin tilted, and her eyes became dark, gold-flecked obsidian. 'For this, you require proof of paternity?'

'A considerable fortune is involved.'

Sufficient to put Nicki on a spoilt-little-rich-girl list and all that entailed.

'No.'

'It is her right as a Martinez heir.'

'Never sure of being liked for herself, or for who she is and what she can do for them? Living in a gilded cage, guarded and protected? Unable to enjoy the freedom of a normal childhood?'

Marcello drained his coffee and signalled the waitress for another, indicating only one when Shannay shook her head.

'Wealth brings risks. Bodyguards are discreet. It's something one learns to live with.'

She made a sweeping glance of the area, then returned her attention to him. 'Next, you'll tell me *yours* is seated near by.' It was a comment veiled with deliberate cynicism, and she caught the slight twist at the edge of his mouth.

'Three tables to your right. Tall, dark hair, shades, dressed in jeans and polo shirt. Carlo doubles as my personal assistant.'

So much for flippancy.

She hadn't sensed anyone's presence, or felt that inexplicable prickling at the back of her neck…and she definitely hadn't *seen* anything to arouse suspicion.

But then, the possibility hadn't occurred to her. She was here in Perth, Australia. A woman and her young daughter living a normal life.

Far, far removed from Madrid and the Martinez lifestyle where protection of its family members formed an integral part of their existence.

She was all too aware of Marcello's veiled scrutiny, the watching quality as he gauged her mood, divined it, then closed in for the kill.

'Sign the permission form, Shannay. Apply for Nicki's passport, and request urgency on the grounds overseas travel is imminent.'

A chill shiver slithered its way down her spine. Without a passport Nicki was confined within Australia.

Once a passport was issued, her daughter would be able to travel…anywhere, independent of her mother.

The mere thought escalated her nervous tension and sent her mind spiralling with very real fear of abduction…by Marcello, if he was so inclined to take Nicki to Madrid, with or without Shannay's permission.

Something she'd fight to guard against, at any cost.

'Or else you'll drag me through the courts, Marcello?'

'Why not view a sojourn in Madrid as an opportunity for Nicki to become accustomed to my home, my family, and to enjoy aspects of the city in the security of your company?'

She knew what would follow, and he didn't disappoint.

'Ramon will have time with his great-grand-daughter. Is that too much to ask of you?'

'And how is this *holiday* to be explained to Nicki? She's intelligent for her age. She'll ask questions, expect answers.'

'Why not lead her into the truth a step at a time?'

Shannay viewed him with scepticism. 'A suggestion from a man who has no experience with children?'

'Is it so difficult to accept such a suggestion might have some merit?'

'I'm all ears,' she evinced with deliberate mockery.

'Not to mention doubtful and prejudiced.'

Her eyes flashed chips of gold fire. 'With good reason.'

'Let's focus on the current issue, shall we?'

'Oh, by all means.'

He wanted to take hold of her fire and change it to passion, to still the anger and have her sigh beneath the touch of his mouth, his hands. To come alive and move with him, savour the anticipation, the slow emotive path to sensual ecstasy they had once enjoyed.

And would again. He intended to make certain of it.

For the challenge…and for revenge.

'Allow Nicki to know I'm a relative of Ramon. It will explain why I am escorting you both to visit him in Madrid.'

'You think Ramon will go along with that?'

'I know so.'

'And Penè?' Shannay gave a laugh of cynical disbelief.

'Penè will conform,' Marcello declared hardily.

'Sure, and cows jump over the moon!'

'Your analogy amuses me.'

'But…*apt.*'

'You seem to forget I control the Martinez finances, from which Penè is allocated a very generous contribution to suit her preferred lifestyle.'

She got it. And knew he was sufficiently ruthless to enforce the threat should his aunt choose to ignore his wishes.

'Perhaps you'll explain when you intend Nicki should know—'

'I'm her father?' Marcello intervened. 'When the right moment occurs.'

Which possibly might not be during their few weeks in Madrid. It even seemed feasible, for she and Nicki would obviously be staying in hotel accommodation, and making daily calls to see Ramon…whose illness would preclude lengthy visits.

There would be time to show Nicki some of the cultural aspects of her paternal heritage, to explore and have fun. It would be so easy to give in. And she almost did. Except there were still matters needing clarification.

'What's the catch, Marcello?'

'Why should you think there is one?'

His voice was too mild, too neutral. 'I have reason to be wary of your motives.'

'While I have been nothing but honest with you.'

Shannay regarded him carefully, seeing the latent power apparent, and chose to play a few cards of her own.

'Before I'll agree to anything,' she voiced with quiet determination, 'you need to furnish notarised documentation stating a custody schedule for the next two years, subject to my approval and renewable at my discretion.'

His expression didn't change. 'Perhaps you'll offer some indication what arrangements you find acceptable?'

'Nicki can spend two weeks with you, twice a year.' It was so small a concession it was almost pathetic. 'While you, of course, are welcome to visit her in Perth as frequently as your business interests permit.'

'Those are your terms?' His query was silk-smooth and almost deadly.

'There's one more thing. Return airline tickets in Nicki's and my names, and accommodation for two weeks.'

'Three.'

'Excuse me?'

'Three weeks. Airline tickets are unnecessary. We'll travel in my private jet.'

She barely managed to hold back a choked laugh. How could she have neglected to remember the private jet? 'In that case, one-way tickets from Madrid to Perth.'

'Specify a date, and I'll ensure the jet is available for your return.'

Shannay rose to her feet, retrieved a note to cover the cost of her latte, and slid it beneath the saucer.

A gesture of independence, she assured silently as she caught up her wallet. 'I'll print up a copy of everything we've discussed and give it to you when we meet at the park.' She cast her watch a quick glance, and was surprised at the passage of time.

Without a further word she turned and retraced her steps to the apartment building, aware of the strange feeling in the pit of her stomach.

She'd expected Marcello to argue her terms, even dismiss them out of hand.

Why hadn't he?

Because he'd achieved his objective…her permission for Nicki to meet Ramon Martinez, patriarch of the Martinez dynasty.

Yet *she* had set the boundaries.

What was more, she'd insisted on a number of specific conditions to be set down in notarised legalese. Plus Nicki's passport would remain in Shannay's possession for the entire sojourn, she'd make sure of that.

All contingencies taken care of, she decided with satisfaction as she printed out two copies, closed down the laptop, then she collected a cool-pack filled with fresh fruit and drinks, caught up her bag and took the lift down to basement level.

Nicki's excitement was palpable as Shannay collected her from kindergarten and drove towards the park.

Yes, she assured, they were on time.

Yes, she'd remembered to bring a packet of sliced bread to feed the ducks.

And yes, she was sure Marcello knew where to meet them.

The park was a popular spot, and there were several couples and families relaxing on the grassy banks overlooking the water.

It was a beautiful early summer's day, with the whisper of a breeze teasing the heavily leaf-laden trees as Shannay selected a pleasant spot and spread a picnic rug on the ground.

'I think he's here,' Nicki announced breathlessly minutes later. 'Yes, it's him.' She raised her arms and waved to attract his attention.

Smile, Shannay bade silently as Marcello joined them, and she buried the faint resentment at just how easily her daughter appeared to be falling beneath his spell.

As picnics went, it was a tremendous success...from Nicki's perspective.

The *best,* Nicki accorded with enthusiasm as she recounted every high point...and there were many, mostly centred around Marcello.

There was no doubt about the mutual attraction developing between father and child. Nicki's giggles and unaffected laughter testified to it. So too did the unguarded affection Marcello displayed for his daughter.

He was a natural, Shannay had to admit, unsure how she felt about their burgeoning bond.

Dammit, it had to be a good thing, she allowed as she drove to work later that afternoon.

If she repeated the words often enough, maybe she'd begin to believe them.

The signed notarised document was already in her possession, courtesy of express courier delivery. Perusal clarified it duplicated the print-out she'd handed Marcello during lunch.

Attached had been a contact name and number to expedite the issue of Nicki's passport.

By week's end, they should be able to leave for Madrid.

Providing she adhered to their agreement, countersigned the notarised document, signed the DNA paternity permission form, lodged the necessary passport documentation and arranged leave of absence from her place of work.

An exceedingly efficient set of suggestions offered to hasten their departure.

Instructions, Shannay corrected, under no illusion they

were anything other than Marcello's ability to use his wealth and influence to achieve his objective.

There was a part of her that understood his motives, together with a degree of sympathy for an ailing elderly man wanting to see his only great-grandchild.

She'd covered all her bases...hadn't she?

And three weeks was hardly a lifetime.

So why did she feel this faint niggle of apprehension?

It stayed with her as she worked, although she deliberately consigned it to the back of her mind as she gave her full attention to dispensing prescriptions, greeting and conversing with patients and customers frequenting the pharmacy.

There was the usual early-evening rush, followed by a lull, during which she had the opportunity to request a leave of absence.

John Bennett, the owner of the pharmacy who was both employer and friend, paused from his task of checking stock and gave Shannay his full attention.

'This is a bit sudden. Care to provide the reason?'

Shannay offered the bare minimum, aware he filled in the blanks himself.

'You consider this a wise move, Shannay?'

John was a nice man, caring and pleasant to work with. He also wanted to date her...something she refused to do. She liked him, but...and it was the *but* that mattered.

Friendship was fine, but not a relationship. With John, it could only be the latter and she wouldn't contemplate taking that step.

'It's an amicable one.' At least I'm being led to believe it is, she added silently. 'And I've taken precautionary protective measures.'

'Such as?'

Shannay crossed to her bag, extracted the notarised agreement and handed it to him, watchful of his expression as he read the contents.

'You want my honest opinion?'

'Of course.'

John folded the paperwork and passed it back to her.

'My main concern is whether, if contested, it would stand up in a court of law.' He paused. 'Do you trust him?'

Trust encompassed much. 'With Nicki's welfare. Yes.'

'And with yours?' he persisted quietly.

I don't know. 'It's only three weeks, John.'

'If you're sure.'

Sure? How could she be sure of anything that involved Marcello? They had a chequered history, one of extreme highs and lows.

A roller-coaster ride, she added silently, and stilled the sensual curl threatening to unfurl deep within her memory of what they'd shared…during the good times.

The evening followed its usual pattern, with a busy period as the nearby cinema-plex emptied and the occasional parent desperate for nursery supplies made a hurried trip to the dispensary.

It was almost closing time when the electronic door buzzer announced a last-minute arrival. Shannay checked the security-cam, and felt the breath catch in her throat as she saw Marcello moving towards the counter.

Gone were the chinos and collarless shirt he'd worn during the day. Tailored trousers, an open-necked shirt and jacket adorned his strong masculine body.

'I'll close up.'

Shannay heard John's words, and quickly turned towards

him, then she gathered herself together sufficiently to effect an introduction.

'What are you doing here, and why now?' she asked quietly as John moved towards the front entrance.

'Whatever happened to *hello?*' Marcello drawled, watching as she efficiently checked data on the computer, then closed down.

'You were in the area and thought you'd call in?' She lifted an eyebrow. 'Or primarily to collect paperwork which I have yet to sign?'

'Both,' he concurred smoothly. 'I'm sure John won't object to witnessing your signature.'

Shannay was tempted to provide further delaying tactics, just for the hell of it. Except such an action would be retaliatory and pointless.

It didn't take long, and Marcello slid the paperwork into his jacket pocket, then waited while she pulled on a jacket and caught up her bag.

She didn't particularly want him to accompany her out into the cool night air.

He…affected her, and she wasn't comfortable with it. Any more than she felt at ease witnessing John's silent reticence in Marcello's presence.

There shouldn't *be* this faintly breathless sense of sexual energy attacking the fragile tenure of her control.

It made her feel slightly off-balance, aware of him at some tenuous level that threatened to shift the foundations she'd fought so hard to cement during the past few years.

Crazy, she dismissed. She was tired, that was all, and tense. Worse, she was allowing her imagination to run riot.

She shot him a cursory look as they reached the front of the pharmacy. 'I have my own car.'

'You object to me ensuring you reach it safely?'

His mild query elicited a faintly derisive dismissal. 'You're being ridiculous.'

They walked out into darkness where illumination was provided by distant streetlights and a sickle moon.

He was too close. Within touching distance, and the faint aroma of his cologne teased her senses, together with the male scent that was his alone.

Her car was parked in full view, and she deactivated the alarm, paused as Marcello opened the door, then she quickly slid in behind the wheel.

He held the door and leaned down towards her. 'I'll be in touch.'

Shannay inclined her head, fired the engine and sent the sedan out onto the road in the direction of home.

CHAPTER FIVE

THE LUXURIOUSLY FITTED Gulf Stream jet cruised at a diminishing altitude as it began its descent to Barajas Airport.

A long flight, during which Shannay had plenty of time to reflect…and wonder for the umpteenth time *why* she'd agreed to leave the relative security of her own territory for a city in a country which held so many conflicting memories for her, not all of them good.

Carlo's presence helped ease the intimacy of so few passengers sharing the cabin, and he was a pleasant man in his early forties, tall, whipcord-lean and alert in a way that behoved his position.

It will be fine, she silently reassured.

She was in control, she'd covered every contingency, and this was only a very temporary visit to Madrid.

Nicki travelled well, in awe of her surroundings, the flight, and was almost heartbreakingly willing to please.

Marcello had become Nicki's new best friend during the week it had taken to confirm his paternity and complete travel documentation.

There had been only one awkward moment when Nicki had asked Marcello in childish innocence, 'Are you my uncle?'

'I'm related to the Spanish side of your family,' he'd responded gently, and solemn young eyes viewed him with un-blinking regard.

'Do you know my daddy?'

'Yes, I do.'

'Will I meet him?'

Oh, dear heaven, *don't*. Not now, not yet, Shannay silently beseeched.

'I can promise you will.'

The undisguised rapport they shared had to be a good thing, Shannay constantly reminded herself as she bit down her reaction to the gentle patience he displayed with their daughter.

It made her think of other times when *she* had delighted in the touch of his hand, his warm smile…and his love.

For it had been *love* in all its various facets, when she'd believed nothing could rend it asunder.

Yet it had, and being in his company, returning to Madrid, brought everything back into vivid focus.

She could deal with it. She had to, for Nicki's sake.

Her daughter's happiness, contentment and security were paramount.

So…get over it.

The jet touched down smoothly, completed the allotted runway, then slid into a designated bay where they disem-barked, Marcello dealt with their baggage and formalities before directing them to a waiting limousine bearing the discreet but influential Martinez emblem.

Madrid temperatures in October were not too dissimilar to the early-summer temperatures in Perth. A pleasant time of year in both cities, neither too hot nor too cold.

Shannay saw Nicki seated in the centre of the rear seat, then slid in beside her, aware Marcello gained access on Nicki's right.

He'd showered, shaved and changed clothes during the flight, so too had she, and, while she'd lain down with Nicki in the bedroom compartment, sleep had come only in brief snatches.

The drive into the city's heart would take slightly less than half an hour. She had little concern about Marcello's choice of hotel accommodation…only an impending sense of relief that their arrival would provide escape from his company at least until the next day.

He might be accustomed to changing time zones on a regular basis, but both she and Nicki were not.

Madrid, a city of splendid architecture, combining a fascinating mix of the old and modern, the cacophony of sounds, traffic, voices in a language she hadn't heard spoken in almost four years.

Shannay felt the light press of Nicki's fingers curled within her own, and examined her daughter's features as she took intent interest in the passing scene beyond the lightly tinted windows.

'It's different,' Nicki said tentatively.

'The traffic travels in the opposite way from where you live. Soon it will become familiar,' he assured, and met Shannay's faintly lifted eyebrow.

In a three-week time-frame? I don't think so.

A faint smile tugged the edges of his mouth as he transferred his attention to Nicki. 'Not much longer, *pequena,* and we will be there.'

Nicki regarded him solemnly. 'What did you call me?'

'*Pequena,*' he said gently. 'It's an affectionate name for a little girl.'

She tried it out, copying his intonation, and his smile broadened with gentle warmth as he complimented her, resulting in a beam of childish delight.

They were bonding well…and that had to be a good thing, Shannay accepted. So why did it hurt so much?

She met his gaze, attempted to read his expression, failed miserably, and transferred her attention to the scene beyond the limousine window.

Marcello did *enigmatic* very well.

What did she expect? For his expressed warmth towards her in Nicki's presence to contain a grain of genuine emotion?

Please.

She didn't feel a thing for him. *Did she?*

Whatever was causing her heart to quicken its beat, or the butterflies having a ball in her stomach, was merely tension. The stress of ensuring Nicki's emotional welfare remained on an even keel.

Nearly four years' absence had wrought few changes, and a slight frown creased her forehead when the limousine branched off the main arterial route leading into the city.

It took a few kilometres for her tension to escalate as suspicion finally dawned.

No. Please, *please* let me be wrong.

Shannay kept her voice light, when inwardly she was beginning to silently seethe. 'Where are you taking us, Marcello?'

'My home in La Moraleja.'

She shot him a look that inaudibly expressed *you have to be joking*. 'A hotel suite would be more convenient.'

'Ensuring difficulty in enforcing necessary security measures.'

His voice held a degree of steely purpose she couldn't fail to recognise…as he had meant her to.

Her eyes sparked anger as they clashed with his, and if she could have hit him, she'd have lashed out and to hell with the consequences.

Except Nicki was closeted between them, blissfully unaware of her mother's rapidly mounting anger.

But wait, just *wait,* her scathing look silently promised, until I get you alone, behind closed doors and well out of Nicki's hearing.

It was difficult to maintain a sense of calm during the time it took to reach La Moraleja, one of Madrid's exclusive and luxurious suburbs.

Marcello's home was a testament to his wealth and position. Set in beautiful grounds, behind high walls and guarded by electronic gates, the mansion stood as a craftsmen's masterpiece of rambling structural design combining two levels in cream stucco, a cream and terracotta-tiled roof and large curved windows with folding doors, most of which opened out onto a wide terracotta-tiled forecourt.

The entrance was amazing with huge double wood-panelled doors studded in polished brass, reached from a *porte cochère* whose floor featured an exquisite detailed design in marble, accented in polished brass.

She told herself she didn't want to be here. Didn't want to be reminded of the painful memories…or the good ones.

It was too personal, too painful, and *too much.*

Marcello had to know how being here would impact on her.

A house with rooms where they'd argued, fought, made love…

Yet it would become Nicki's temporary home for designated periods of time throughout the year.

Years, she corrected mentally. A place her daughter needed to familiarise herself with, feel welcome in, comfortable.

Being here *now* made sense…for Nicki.

For Shannay, it represented a torture that would stretch her nerves to breaking point over the next three weeks.

He knew it, had planned it, and had deliberately kept her in the dark.

For that he would pay…big time, she vowed as she stepped from the limousine and accompanied Nicki into the large formal foyer where they were greeted by Maria and Emilio, trusted staff of Marcello's who lived in and took care of the house and grounds.

Marble floors, a sweeping staircase, which curved elegantly to the upper floor, a glittering crystal chandelier against a backdrop of coloured patterned glass.

Antique furniture rested against cream walls on which hung original works of art, interspersed with decoratively corniced mini-alcoves displaying an eclectic mix of exquisite vases, bowls and Venetian glassware.

The mansion bore two wings separated by a wide oval balustraded gallery…one designed for formal entertaining with a large dining room, lounge, gourmet kitchen on the first level, while the upper floor held a large study, adjoining library, entertainment room and informal lounge. The west wing comprised three formal guest suites separated by an informal lounge on the first level, with five private suites reposing on the upper level.

The grounds held an infinity pool, a cabana, a well-equipped gym and a tennis court. There were separate self-contained staff quarters built above a large six-car garage.

A large home for one man, Shannay reflected…aware he used it as his main base in between frequent flights to various major cities in various European countries, wheeling and dealing as head of the Martinez corporation.

Marcello's personal portfolio was enviable, providing him with billionaire status in a business world frequented by the ruthless drive for power.

Shannay wondered if he continued to entertain on a regular basis, whether he was active on the social scene and continued to support a few selected charities.

In four years there had to have been at least a few women in his life. Imagining Marcello as a celibate was beyond the bounds of credibility.

Which inevitably led to Marcello's former lover…and Shannay's nemesis. Estella de Cordova.

Was the *über* socialite still on the scene?

And if so, did Marcello intend to marry Estella after they divorced?

A cold hand clutched her heart and squeezed mercilessly *hard*.

Please, dear God, *no*.

The thought Estella might have any part in Nicki's welfare was enough to make Shannay want to throw up.

'You've had a long flight,' Maria began quietly. 'I have tea and some light food prepared. Afterwards, perhaps you would like to rest.'

Carlo brought in their bags and took them upstairs.

'Tea would be lovely. Perhaps a glass of milk for Nicki,' Shannay suggested as Marcello indicated the staircase.

'First, I'll show you to your rooms.'

A personal escort? Somehow she expected him to disappear into his home office.

'It's a big house,' Nicki voiced quietly as they reached the upper level. 'Do other people live here?'

'Sometimes there are guests,' Marcello said gently, meeting her dark, solemn gaze.

'Like Mummy and me.'

'Yes.'

Shannay felt her stomach execute a slow somersault as he

turned away from the wing containing the guest suites and moved down the opposite passage.

She knew the family wing well. Elegant suites, beautifully furbished and furnished.

Did Marcello sleep alone in the master suite, or had he chosen another?

Whoa. Where had that come from?

As if she cared where he slept…as long as it was in a suite far from the one Maria had prepared for herself and Nicki.

The master suite rose vividly in her mind. Positioned at the far end of the family wing, it comprised a large bedroom, two *en suites,* two walk-in wardrobes and an adjoining room containing comfortable deep-seated chairs, a sofa, reading lamps.

Had he had the suite redecorated?

'No.'

Shannay heard his soft drawl and refused to look at him, hating that he still retained the ability to read her mind.

He paused at an open door. 'I think you'll be comfortable here.'

Here was two bedrooms separated by an *en suite,* with one of the bedrooms decorated especially for a young girl. Different shades of pink, from the palest shade to watermelon. Prints hung on the walls, toys in abundance, and the bed was fit for a princess.

Nicki's room.

Shannay got it.

A room that was Nicki's alone, for whenever she visited. A suite she would become familiar with, feel comfortable in and look forward to occupying.

Not too far in distance from where Marcello slept while she was young, so she would feel secure, knowing he was within calling distance.

There was a part of her that hated him for deliberately setting the scene for Nicki's future.

Yet there was also a feeling of gratitude that she didn't want to acknowledge. Together with a mounting anxiety that played havoc with her emotions.

'Is this where I'll sleep?'

Nicki's voice held a degree of wondrous awe.

'Yes.' Marcello moved towards the *en suite,* opened the connecting door and crossed to the opposite door which led into an adjoining bedroom. 'Your mother will sleep here.'

'Can the doors stay open?' Nicki queried tentatively, and he offered a reassuring smile.

'Of course.'

Nicki caught hold of her mother's hand. 'Aren't we lucky?' she said simply, to which Shannay could only answer in the affirmative.

'Marcello is kind to let us stay here.'

She could think of numerous descriptive adjectives…not one of them remotely resembled *kind,* given he had his own agenda.

Their luggage stood at the end of the bed, and Marcello indicated both suitcases. 'Maria will unpack for you. Freshen up, then come downstairs.'

He gave Nicki a warm smile, extended it towards Shannay, then he turned and left the room.

Unpacking would take only a matter of minutes, and Shannay tended to her own, then she transferred Nicki's clothes into the connecting bedroom.

A short while later she accompanied Nicki downstairs to the informal lounge, where Maria served tea, delicate sandwiches and a bowl of freshly cut fruit.

Dinner would be served late…way past Nicki's usual

bedtime, and Shannay decided sandwiches and a glass of milk would suffice as an evening meal on this occasion.

Marcello's presence was unexpected. For some reason she had imagined he'd disappear into his home office and remain there until dinner. A meal she intended to skip on the pretext of bathing Nicki and settling her to sleep.

The flight had been long, his company a constant, and she desperately needed a break from him.

Nicki ate little, drank her milk and began to visibly droop.

'If you'll excuse us?' Shannay took hold of her daughter's hand. 'Say goodnight, darling.'

Nicki politely obliged, and Marcello surprised them both by lifting the young child into his arms.

'I can take her.' She reached out, expecting Nicki to lean towards her…except her daughter remained where she was.

She told herself she wasn't hurt. Silently assured herself it didn't matter. But it did.

Nicki's head had tucked in against the curve of his throat as they reached the bedroom, and he gently lowered her down onto the bed.

'Thanks.' It was a polite, perfunctory gesture that didn't fool him in the slightest.

His eyes seared her own. 'I'll see you at dinner.'

'I'd prefer to remain close to Nicki in case she wakes.'

He regarded her steadily. 'There's a monitor in her room, and auditory receptive devices in every room in the house.' His gaze didn't waver. 'Dinner will be served in two hours. Plenty of time for you to bathe and settle her to sleep before you join me.'

Shannay longed to tell him to go jump. She was on edge, angry, and feeling the effects of jet lag. The thought of sharing a meal with him held no appeal whatsoever.

Yet it would provide the opportunity to vent…and she so badly needed to vent!

He leant down and brushed his lips to Nicki's temple.

'Sleep well, *pequena*.' He straightened, sent Shannay a piercing look, then he turned and left the room.

She had the childish desire to pull a face behind his back, except she restrained herself and tended to her daughter.

Two hours and five minutes later she descended the stairs and made her way towards the informal dining room.

Five minutes over time was acceptable, and in her case deliberate, for she refused to conform to every one of Marcello's dictates.

She'd chosen to wear a black singlet top over which she wore a fine lace black blouse tied at her waist, pencil-slim black skirt, black stilettos, hair pulled back into a French twist secured by a jewelled comb, a slim gold bracelet, understated make-up and lipgloss.

Dressed to kill was an adequate description.

Ready for battle was more apt!

Marcello was waiting for her as she entered the dining room, and one look at him was enough to set the pulse at her throat thrum to a faster beat.

Attired in black tailored trousers, a white chambray shirt, his casual appearance belied the almost barbaric handsomeness of the man.

Strength and power, a degree of ruthlessness made for a dangerous mix she had every reason to view with caution.

Yet there was so much banked-up resentment and anger towards him, it took leashed control to avoid launching into attack mode.

Play nice…for now, she reminded herself silently.

Appear to enjoy a few sips of excellent vintage wine, be

polite through the starter, aim for neutrality as they sampled the main course, then open the verbal discourse over coffee.

That was the plan.

'Shannay.' His voice was a lazy, faintly accented drawl, and she unconsciously lifted her chin.

'Marcello.'

'Can I get you something to drink?'

Civility. She could do that. 'A light medium white, thank you.'

He crossed to a storage cabinet, extracted the appropriate bottle, opened it, poured a quantity into a crystal goblet and extended it towards her.

'Nicki settled well?'

She was careful to avoid his fingers as she took the goblet from his hand. 'Yes. Thank you.'

'So polite, Shannay?'

Her eyes sparked shards of golden fire. 'I thought we'd feign peace and leave war until after dinner.' Her chin lifted a little. 'I have respect for my digestion.'

His soft laughter was almost her undoing as he indicated the table set with fine china, silver flatware and no less than three crystal goblets. 'Let's eat, shall we?'

Maria had surpassed herself with a delicate starter, followed by a seafood paella steaming aromatically beneath a covered serving dish.

'Ramon is anxious to meet Nicki,' Marcello informed as he touched the rim of his goblet to her own in a silent salute. 'How do you feel about tomorrow?'

'Perhaps it could be delayed by a day?' Shannay countered. 'Nicki has had to absorb a lot in the past week, followed by a long flight.' She made a sweeping gesture with her hand to indicate his home. 'All of this.'

'I'll make arrangements.'

It was happening, the increase in Marcello's control to the detriment of her own.

Ramon she could cope with…even look forward to reconnecting with the generous elderly man.

Ramon's daughter, Penè, however, was a different matter. Ramon's son, Marcello and Sandro's father, had been killed instantly in a car crash when Marcello had been in his late teens.

Nicki was the bonus…the one bright star in the Martinez firmament. No one, not even Penè, would be permitted to say a word out of place in Nicki's hearing.

Shannay sampled the starter, and insisted on a small portion of paella. She'd grown unused to eating so late, and she merely sipped her wine, choosing instead to drink chilled water, and declined dessert or coffee.

'Finish your wine.'

She met his faintly hooded gaze with equanimity. 'I prefer to have a clear head.'

Marcello sank back in his chair and regarded her with interest. 'To indulge in verbal warfare?'

'You doubt it?' She barely hid an edge of bitterness in her voice. 'I specifically requested our own accommodation.'

'Yet I have provided accommodation, have I not?' he offered reasonably.

Far more luxurious than the most expensive hotel. 'That isn't the point.'

'What *is* the point?'

'You could have asked for my approval.'

One eyebrow lifted in silent mockery. 'And your answer would have been?'

'Not in this lifetime!'

He spread his hands wide. 'Precisely.'

She wanted to throw something at him. Anything to disrupt his chilling air of calm. 'Doesn't it matter that I don't want to be here?'

'In Madrid? This house? Or with me?'

'All of that...and more!' The words tumbled out with vehement ire.

'*Querida.*' His faintly accented drawl curled round her heart and tugged a little. 'Perhaps you should have given thought to informing me of Nicki's existence from the beginning, instead of hoping fate and distance would continue to keep me in ignorance.'

'Don't...call me that.'

'Darling? Lover?' He offered a faint smile. 'But you are both, yes?'

'Not any more. And never again,' Shannay added with angry intent, and attempted to tamp down the vivid images that immediately flooded her mind.

In his bed, *theirs,* she corrected. Naked, beneath him, her thighs wrapped around his waist, urging him on, pleading, begging for the release only he could give...the heat and the passion. Loving him with her heart and her soul. *His...*only his.

'Careful, *amada.* I could view that as a challenge.'

'In a pig's eye,' she managed fiercely, hating his silky indolence. Not to mention the instinctive feeling he was deliberately toying with her.

He regarded her carefully. 'Had I known you were pregnant, I'd have taken the next flight to Perth and dragged you back here.'

As he had done *now,* she perceived. 'It wouldn't have changed my decision to file for divorce.'

His pause was deliberately significant. 'Yet you failed to do so until very recently.'

'It was my choice to avoid all contact with you,' Shannay offered coolly. 'Even via legal channels.' She waited a beat, and aimed the figurative dart. 'Reciprocal, obviously.'

'Yet circumstances have changed.'

Suspicion clouded her eyes. 'What are you implying?'

'There will be no divorce.'

'The hell there won't!'

He shrugged in an expressive negligent gesture. 'Why bother with legalities?'

'It might suit you to conveniently have a wife in another country, but I don't want a husband!'

'Not even the faithful John waiting patiently in the background?'

'He's my boss and a friend. Nothing more.'

'No?' Marcello arched silkily, and watched her temper flare into vibrant life.

'Damn you, *no*.'

His eyes narrowed slightly. 'Almost four years, Shannay, and you haven't welcomed another man into your bed?'

She wanted to pick something up and throw it at him.

'Don't,' Marcello warned softly. 'I might seek retribution.'

'Bite me.'

'What an interesting concept.' His lazy drawl held amusement…and something else.

'Go to hell.' She hated the faint shakiness in her voice.

She wanted to leave…the room, this house, *him*.

Yet leaving would amount to an admission of sorts, and she refused to give Marcello the satisfaction.

Besides, there was Nicki. And for her daughter, she'd lay down her life. Without askance, or question.

'Not a very comfortable place to be, wouldn't you agree?'

Shannay closed her eyes, then opened them again as she

flashed him a look of gold-flecked enmity. 'Let's balance the scales, shall we?' Her voice held a darkness she didn't know she possessed. 'Or is the list of willing women anxious to share your bed too extensive to recall?'

'You have a vivid imagination, *mi mujer.*'

My wife. She didn't need or want the reminder. 'With just cause.'

'Something, if you remember,' he drawled, 'I refuted at the time.'

Her gaze remained steady. 'You were very credible, Marcello, in light of the facts.'

One eyebrow rose in a gesture of distaste. 'The fabrication of a disturbed woman?'

'We've been there, done that,' Shannay said in a dismissive tone. 'It's old ground.'

'Consign it to the *too hard* basket, and not seek a resolution?'

'There's nothing to resolve.'

'Yet it had a drastic effect on our lives and eroded what we once shared.'

Destroyed it, she wanted to fling at him...and knew she lied. The sensual pull was as strong now as it had ever been. Almost as if her soul reached out to his in a pagan call as old as time.

She could feel it, sense it deep inside, stirring to life in damning recognition.

Why? she demanded silently. And why now?

Tension. Stress. Jet lag.

A lethal combination which attacked her vulnerability, she justified without conviction.

'I'm over it.' It took tremendous effort to say the words, but she achieved them...barely.

She'd had enough, and her nerves were stretched to breaking

point. With a careful movement she rose to her feet and held the dark, gleaming gaze of the inimical man seated opposite.

'I'm going to bed.'

She turned, and had taken only a few steps when she heard the quiet silky timbre of his voice.

'For the record…we're not done.'

Her stomach jolted at the thinly veiled threat, and it was only through sheer strength of will she didn't falter.

Seconds later she reached the wide arched doorway, and she sensed the faint mockery as he bade,

'Sleep well.'

CHAPTER SIX

SHANNAY CAME AWAKE slowly, stretched a little, reached for her watch to check the time and gave a gasp of dismay.

Nicki.

She flung back the covers, caught up her robe and hurried through the *en suite* to the adjoining bedroom, felt her heart leap to her throat at the sight of Nicki's bed neatly made and no sign of her daughter.

Where…?

It was then she caught sight of the note propped against the pillow, and she hurriedly snatched it up, read the brief script in bold black ink, "Nicki downstairs in Maria's care," and felt the panic begin to subside.

All it took was ten minutes to shower, pull on dress jeans and a casual top over bra and briefs, slide her feet into heeled sandals, then she made her way down to the informal dining room to greet a glowing Nicki being fussed over by the benevolent Maria.

'Marcello said not to wake you,' the housekeeper relayed as she poured steaming aromatic coffee into a cup, offered a wide choice of food for breakfast and shook her head slightly when Shannay chose fresh fruit and yoghurt.

'It's mid-morning,' Shannay reminded with a wry smile. 'My body clock needs time to adjust.'

'Marcello said we can go to a park after lunch,' Nicki informed as Shannay took a seat at the table.

'That's nice.' What else could she say? Any hope Marcello might absent himself in his city office each day seemed doomed. Which meant any form of freedom wasn't going to happen.

Goodbye to checking out theme parks as carefree tourists. No spur-of-the-moment shopping excursions.

This was Madrid. Here she was affiliated to the Martinez family, where extreme wealth necessitated due care with a bodyguard in attendance beyond the safety of home.

She hadn't liked it then. Any more than she did now. Except there was Nicki, with little or no conception of her true identity...yet. A vulnerable child who hadn't been groomed almost from birth to always be aware of possible danger, to unquestionably obey the people in charge of her welfare, or having been taught simple but vital diversionary survival tactics.

It was a heavy load for such a young child, and not something instantly learned.

Although she was loath to admit Marcello had been right in bringing them into his home, it made perfect sense to utilise their three-week sojourn as a learning curve.

It was no use wishing fate hadn't had a hand in bringing Nicki's existence to Sandro and Luisa's attention.

Life was filled with coincidence, occasionally against all the odds...and she had to deal with it.

Shannay finished her breakfast, drained the rest of her coffee and extended a hand towards her daughter.

'Shall we go explore?'

The house first, then the grounds...with Carlo in attendance at a reasonable distance when they ventured outdoors.

High walls, electronic gates, sophisticated security monitoring the grounds.

Together she and Nicki trod the neat paths as they viewed the immaculate lawns, the gardens with their beautiful flowerbeds providing brilliant colour, carefully tended shrubbery precision-clipped to landscaped perfection.

'It's pretty,' Nicki announced, then pointed in excitement. 'There's a swimming pool. Are we allowed to swim in it?'

'Only when I'm with you,' she cautioned firmly.

'Or Marcello?'

Shannay inclined an agreement, and felt a degree of maternal alarm at the thought of Nicki being left unsupervised when she wasn't around. Then she calmed down a little. For the next two years, Nicki's sojourns here would be restricted to a few...except how could she ever learn to let go?

She'd be a nervous wreck from the time her daughter boarded the jet until she returned to Australian soil.

'It's a very big house,' Nicki declared, visibly awed by the luxurious interior as they moved through the various rooms.

Shannay provided a running explanation as they completed the first level and trod the stairs to the upper level.

'I like our wing best,' Nicki clutched a tighter hold of Shannay's hand, ''specially my room.'

Who wouldn't?

Marcello joined them for lunch, and from his casual attire he'd obviously conducted the morning's work in his home office.

Black jeans, a white shirt unbuttoned at the neck and the long sleeves rolled back at the cuffs, he resembled a dark angel, rugged with his hair less smoothly groomed than usual...almost as if he'd thrust fingers through its thickness in exasperation. And if so, why?

In the early days of their marriage she would have walked up to him, cupped his broad facial features between both hands and leaned in to savour the touch of his mouth. Feel his arms close round her slim body as he deepened the kiss, and exult in his arousal.

A time when she'd thought nothing could damage their love. How naive had she been?

'Must I have a nap?'

Shannay caught the subdued excitement bubbling beneath the surface as Nicki silently pleaded with her.

'Uh-huh.' She tempered it with a smile, hating the disappointment clouding her daughter's expressive features. 'Everyone has a siesta after lunch.'

Nicki's eyes grew round with surprise. 'Even grown-ups?' She looked at Marcello. 'You, too?'

'Sometimes, if I'm home and not too busy.' His smile transformed his features, and Shannay felt the familiar sensation curl deep within in memory of how they'd shared the afternoon siesta when *sleep* hadn't been a factor.

Marcello's sanction made it OK, and Nicki obediently caught hold of Shannay's hand as she led her daughter upstairs to her room.

With outer clothes removed and tucked beneath light covers, Nicki fell asleep within minutes, and Shannay moved through to her own room, too restless to do other than flick through a magazine.

No matter how hard she tried, she couldn't shake an instinctively inexplicable feeling of impending…*what?*

She shook her head in exasperation, then dispensed with the magazine. It was crazy. *She* was crazy.

It was mid-afternoon when Carlo brought the expensive Porsche four-wheel-drive to the front door, and with Nicki happily ensconced in the rear seat between Shannay and Marcello they headed for the nearest park.

Her daughter's enthusiasm for everything new appeared boundless, and she watched as Nicki explored, frequently calling for Marcello to come look at a butterfly, a bee, a pretty flower.

By day's end, fed and bathed, Nicki contentedly settled in bed as Marcello read her a bedtime story, then when he reached the end he brushed a light kiss to his daughter's forehead, bade her goodnight and left the room.

Shannay adjusted the night-light, checked the internal monitor, and when she turned Nicki was already breathing evenly in sleep.

If she could, she'd request a tray in her room in lieu of dinner. Except it would be seen as a cop-out, and she refused to allow Marcello to witness so much as a chink in her feminine armour.

Instead, she showered and dressed in an elegant trouser suit, left her hair loose, applied minimum make-up and went down to join Marcello.

A familiar sensation knotted her stomach as she caught sight of his tall, compelling frame, only to tighten considerably as he turned to face her.

There was a degree of lazy arrogance apparent in those dark eyes…a knowledge that probed deep beyond the surface and saw too much.

In the full blush of love, she'd thought it incredibly romantic. Now she viewed it as an aberration.

Once again she declined wine in favour of chilled water, and sought to set the record straight.

'There's no need for you to ignore your social life while Nicki and I are here.'

'Once our daughter is settled for the night I should feel

under no obligation to entertain her mother?' Marcello's voice held a tinge of something she didn't care to define.

'You got it in one.'

'Why would you imagine I'd choose to ignore a guest in my home?'

'Cut the polite verbal word play,' Shannay advised. 'There's no need to insult my intelligence by pretending we're anything other than opposing forces in all areas of our lives.'

'Nicki being the one exception?'

'The *only* exception.'

'But a very important factor, wouldn't you agree?'

He was doing it again, and she glared at him as she took a seat at the table.

'I concede the need to maintain a friendly relationship in Nicki's presence. But rest assured, the less I see of you, the better.'

'Afraid, Shannay?'

'Of you? No.'

'Perhaps you should be,' Marcello warned silkily as he indicated she should help herself to the chicken stew gently steaming in the serving dish.

'Oh, please.' She transferred a small portion of stew onto her plate, replaced the ladle and speared him a glittering look. 'Cut me a break, why don't you?'

He served himself a generous portion, then he selected a fork from the flatware displayed.

'Almost four years,' he drawled. 'Yet the pulse at the base of your throat betrays you with a faster beat.'

'Your ego astounds me.'

'Have you not wondered how our lives would be now had you remained here?'

'Not at all,' she managed coolly, and knew she lied, aware

of the nights she had lain awake imagining that very thing. How their pursuit of happiness had faltered, then fallen apart. Perhaps Nicki wouldn't be the only child she'd bear...because for the life of her she couldn't think of sharing her body with another man or having his child.

'Interesting.'

Shannay carefully folded her linen napkin and placed it on the table, then she rose to her feet and shot him a killing look. 'Go to hell, Marcello.'

'Sit down, Shannay.'

'Only to be picked apart and analysed merely for your amusement? Forget it.'

She turned away from the table and had only taken a few steps when firm hands closed over her shoulders.

In a strictly reactive movement she lifted her head and glared at him. 'What next? Strong-arm tactics?'

'No. Just this.'

He lowered his head down to hers and captured her mouth with his own in a hard kiss that took her by surprise and plundered at will.

The faint cry of distress rose and died in her throat, and almost as if he sensed it his touch gentled a little and became frankly sensual, seeking the sensitive tissues before stroking the edge of her tongue with the tip of his own in a flagrant dance that stirred at the latent passion simmering beneath the surface of her control.

She felt his hands shift as one slid to cup the back of her head, while the other smoothed down her back and brought her close against him.

Her eyelids shuttered down as she fought against capitulation. The temptation to return his kiss was unbearable, and she groaned as he eased back and began a sensual tasting, teasing the soft fullness of her lower lip, nipping a little with the edges of his teeth, until she succumbed to the sweet sorcery he bestowed.

Dear heaven. It was like coming home as he shaped her mouth with his own, encouraging her response, taking her with him in an evocative tasting that became *more*…and promised much.

Her breasts firmed against his chest, their sensitive peaks hardening in need…for the touch of his hand, his mouth, and she whimpered, totally lost in the moment.

The hardness of his erection was a potent force, and warmth raced through her veins, activating each pleasure pulse until she felt so incredibly sensually *alive,* it was almost impossible not to beg.

It was the slide of his hand over the curve of her breast, the way he shaped it, then slid to loosen the buttons that gave her a moment's pause for thought.

It would be so very easy to link her hands behind his neck and silently invite him to rekindle the flame.

And she almost did. *Almost.*

Except sanity and the dawning horror of where this was going provided the impetus to pull away.

What was she doing?

Was she out of her mind?

'I hate you.' The words came out as a tortured whisper as she dropped her arms and attempted to move back a pace.

For what seemed an age Marcello examined her features, the dilated eyes so dark, almost bruised, with passion. The soft, swollen mouth trembling from his possession.

The shocked dismay.

'Perhaps you hate yourself more,' he offered quietly.

For losing control? *Enjoying* his touch?

And, dear lord…wanting it all.

He watched as she straightened her shoulders, tilted her chin and summoned a fiery glare.

'I'm done. And *that*,' she flung recklessly, 'was a ridiculous experiment.'

Marcello let her go, watching as she moved towards the door and exited the room.

Experiment? Far from it.

A mark of intent.

And he was far from done.

The photograph had been taken with a telephoto lens. Had to be, for Shannay couldn't recall seeing a photographer anywhere as they'd disembarked from Marcello's private jet.

Marcello Martinez with a woman and child in tow had sent the news-hounds into a frenzy. How long would it have taken to filch out archival data and discover the woman was Marcello's estranged wife…and determine the child was his own?

Not long.

The caption, even in Spanish, was unmistakable.

How difficult was it to interpret *reconciliacón?*

Or resurrect her knowledge of the language sufficiently to comprehend Señor Martinez' remark, upon being requested to comment?

Anything is possible.

Really?

Anger suffused her body, coalescing into one great tide of fury, taxing her control to the limit.

With care she tore out the offending page, then folded it a few times and slid it into the pocket of her jeans, determined to initiate a confrontation.

He was home…but *where?*

His home office would be the best place to begin.

She sought out Maria, who took one look at the clenched jaw, the blazing eyes, and immediately caught hold of Nicki's hand.

'Come, *pequena,* we will go into the kitchen and bake some biscuits, *si?*'

Shannay even achieved a tense smile. 'Thank you.' She smoothed a hand over Nicki's hair. 'Be good for Maria. I'll check with you soon. OK?'

'OK.'

Marcello's home office was situated in the far corner of the first level, overlooking the gardens and pool area. Two adjoining rooms whose dividing wall had been removed and refurbished to hold a large executive desk, hi-tech computers, a laptop and the requisite office equipment in one half of the room, while floor-to-ceiling bookcases lined the walls of the remaining half, together with a few comfortable leather chairs, lamps and side-tables.

A very male domain, and one she entered with barely an accompanying knock to announce her presence.

Marcello glanced up from a computer screen, caught the gleaming anger apparent in her dark eyes and settled back in his chair to regard her with thoughtful speculation.

Attired in black jeans and a watermelon-pink top, her hair pulled back into a careless pony-tail and no make-up he could discern, she looked little more than a teenager. Harbouring self-righteous anger he was tempted to stir into something more.

Her honest emotions had always intrigued him, for she rarely held back…a quality lacking in many women of his acquaintance. Sophisticated women who played a false seductive game with both eyes on the main chance.

Shannay had been different. She hadn't known who he was, and didn't appear to care when she did.

Four years ago he hadn't been able to prevent her leaving. Hadn't fought for her as he should have done, erroneously supposing all he needed to do to soothe some of the hurt and pain inflicted by Estella and his widowed aunt was provide evidence of his love by gifting sex.

Exceptional lovemaking, he reflected, and felt his body tighten in remembered passion.

'There's something you want to discuss?'

He looked so damned laid-back, controlled. Even, she decided furiously, faintly amused.

With studied calm she extracted the folded newsprint from her pocket, opened it out and tossed it down onto his desk.

'Perhaps you'd care to explain?'

He merely gave it a glance. 'I'm sure your knowledge of the Spanish language is sufficient to provide a reasonably accurate translation.'

The fact he was right didn't sit well. 'That isn't the issue here.'

His eyes never left her face. 'What is the issue, Shannay?'

'A reconciliation was *never* on the cards.' Her eyes flashed gold sparks, and her fingers curled into her palm in frustrated anger. 'There's no way in hell it's going to happen.'

'You think not?'

'I demand you order a retraction.'

'No.' His voice was dangerously soft, his expression an unyielding mask. 'You deny it would be advantageous for Nicki to have two parents, a stable family life, and thus negate custody arrangements in two countries on the opposite sides of the world?'

'With a mother and father constantly at war? *Please.*'

'Would there necessarily need to be dissension?' He made an encompassing gesture with one hand. 'You would enjoy every social advantage and as my wife, be gifted anything you want.'

Marcello watched the fleeting expressions, divined each and every one of them, and moved in for the kill.

'Not even to please a very ill old man with only a short time to live?'

Conflicting emotions tore at her emotional heart and lent shadows to her eyes.

'Ramon has a very progressive form of cancer,' he relayed quietly. 'Various surgical procedures have delayed the inevitable. However, the brain tumour is inoperable, and the medical professionals predict it will only be a matter of weeks before he lapses into a coma.'

Shannay was unable to hide the shock, or her genuine regret. 'I'm so sorry. Why didn't you warn me?'

'I thought I had.'

She searched for the precise words he'd used. 'You said he was ill,' she recalled. 'You didn't say he is dying.'

She was conscious of his scrutiny, the studied ease with which he regarded her as the impact of his words sank in.

'Given the circumstances, is it too much to ask?'

Her eyes held his. 'What about Nicki? Ramon wants to meet her, but have you given a thought to how Ramon's rapidly deteriorating health will affect her? She's only a child, and she's much too young to assimilate and cope with illness of this magnitude.'

'I've agonised over it,' Marcello assured quietly. 'At the moment Ramon spends a short time sitting in a comfortable chair in the *sala*. He looks old, a little tired and fragile, but he's remarkably lucid.' He regarded her thoughtfully. 'You will be able to judge for yourself.' An entire gamut of conflicting emotions vied for supremacy, including doubt. In the end, compassion won out.

'You give me your word you'll allow me to decide when Nicki's visits should cease?'

'Without question.' He sank further back in his chair and raised his hands to cup his nape. 'The purported reconciliation? You'll agree to the pretence for Ramon's sake?'

Why did she harbour the feeling she was being led deeper into deception with every passing day?

She wanted no part of it.

Yet it seemed so little to do to ease an elderly man's mind. To let him believe…what? That his beloved eldest grandson had reconciled with his wife? Spend time with his only great-grandchild?

Couldn't she gift Ramon that much?

'Aren't you forgetting something? *Someone?*' Shannay asked at last.

Marcello didn't pretend to misunderstand.

'Nicki will be told precisely who I am before we visit Ramon.'

'Which will be *when?*'

He checked his watch. 'At eleven.'

Just over an hour? 'Excuse me?'

'You heard.'

Without thought she reached for a paperweight and threw it at him.

Only to miss, as he fielded it in one hand.

For a moment the air was electric, stark and momentous in its silence, and her eyes darkened with horrified disbelief as Marcello placed the glass weight onto the desk, then rose slowly to his feet.

She couldn't move, her feet seemingly cemented to the floor as he crossed to her side.

There wasn't a word she could utter, for her voice couldn't

pierce the lump that had risen in her throat, and she stood powerless as he captured her chin.

His eyes were dark, almost black with forbidding anger, and his voice emerged in husky warning.

'Play with fire, *querida,* and you risk getting burned.'

He ran a finger along the edge of her jaw, almost caressing its shape, and a shiver slithered through her body.

'So much emotion,' Marcello opined silkily. 'Why is that, do you suppose?'

'Because I hate you.'

'Better hate than indifference.'

His fingers curled over her chin as he stroked a thumb over her lower lip…felt it tremble beneath his touch, and offered a faint smile.

'Shall I put it to the test?' He traced the column of her throat with the tip of one finger, rested briefly in the hollow between her breasts, then slid to cup one soft mound and brush its peak with a provocative sweep of his thumb.

She felt it swell and harden beneath his touch, and hated her traitorous reaction.

'Let me go.'

His voice lowered to an indolent purr. 'But we're not yet done.'

His mouth brushed hers in a teasing tracery that almost made her sway, and she stifled a faint groan as he pulled her lower lip between his teeth.

She was hardly aware of the fingers of one hand working the snap at her waist, or the subtle slide of the zip fastening…until she felt his palm against the bare skin of her stomach.

Then it was too late and her startled protest became lost in the way he filled her mouth, and she felt her body jerk spasmodically as his fingers slid through the soft curling hair at the junction of her thighs, then sought and found the moist warmth at her feminine core.

With unerring accuracy he stroked the swollen clitoris and watched the way her eyes glazed as sensation arced through her in an encompassing wave. One which swelled again and again with every tantalising stroke, and he absorbed her cry as he used his fingers in a simulated thrust that sent her high.

He wanted more, much more, and the temptation to take her here, now, was an almost unbearable hunger.

On the desk, the floor, straddling him on the chair, pushed against the wall.

The fact he could acted as a deterrent, and he simply held her, softening the touch of his mouth against her own until the shudders raking her slender form slowed and subsided.

With care he withdrew his hand, closed the zip fastening on her jeans and pressed the snap.

The action brought her back to her senses, and she pushed away from him, unable to believe she'd allowed what had just happened…to *happen*.

How could she have relaxed her guard and become so seduced by his touch…dear heaven, his intrusion?

She didn't want to look at him. Couldn't bear to see the satisfaction evident in his eyes, or his pleasure at her downfall.

For an age neither of them spoke, and the only audible sound in the room was the slightly uneven sound of her breathing.

'That was despicable,' Shannay managed, hating him so much she almost shook with it. She lifted a hand and wiped the back of it across her mouth in an attempt to dispense the taste of him.

And glimpsed the compelling sensuality apparent before he masked his expression.

'But…enlightening, wouldn't you agree?'

'You're keeping score?' she countered with a tinge of bitterness, and saw his expression harden.

'Where is Nicki?'

She took a deep breath and released it slowly. 'In the kitchen with Maria making biscuits.'

'Then let's go get her.'

She looked at him sharply. 'Now?'

Get a grip, why don't you?

How, when her emotions were in turmoil and her body had yet to recover? Even thinking about his touch was enough to cause tiny spasms in the most sensitive part of her anatomy.

'We'll tell her together.'

With an effort she pulled herself together. 'I should be the one—'

'She deserves to have both her parents present.'

Apprehension didn't cover it as they collected Nicki and took her upstairs, and as they neared her room Shannay began doing deals with the deity.

This was major. *Major,* she reiterated silently as Marcello placed Nicki on her bed, and hunkered down to her eye level.

He kept the telling simple. So very simple, it was easy to follow his lead. And Nicki's reaction became a timeless moment, one that caught the heartstrings and plucked the emotional depths as she stood and unhesitatingly wrapped her arms around Marcello's neck.

His eyes burned fiercely over Nicki's head as he hugged her close, and Shannay had to blink hard to prevent the shimmer of tears spilling down her cheeks.

Father and child together.

Nicki's delight and wholehearted acceptance, whose childish words said it all. 'You're my daddy.'

It was a beginning, Shannay acknowledged, for Nicki

was a perceptive child for her age and eventually there would be questions.

But for now, one of the most important hurdles had been conquered.

Marcello pressed a light kiss to his daughter's temple. 'Now we will all get ready to go visit with your *bisabuelo*, Ramon.'

He rested a hand briefly on Shannay's shoulder. 'Fifteen minutes. I'll wait for you downstairs.'

Together they chose Nicki's prettiest dress, and with her hair neatly caught together she followed Shannay into her room as Shannay selected a slim-fitting dress in jade linen, attached a belt, then tended to her hair and make-up beneath her daughter's interested gaze.

Marcello was standing in the foyer as they descended the stairs, and he smiled at Nicki's childish beam when she placed her small hand in his on reaching his side.

Carlo drove through the suburban avenues to Ramon's mansion, parking it in the forecourt immediately adjacent to the main entrance.

Shannay was unprepared for the physical changes in the elderly man, who'd been one of the few Martinez family members to view her kindly before and during her brief marriage to his eldest grandson.

She remembered him as a strong man, despite his advancing years. Vibrant and powerful, yet compassionate to the young woman who'd captured Marcello's heart.

Ramon had encouraged her struggle to learn the Spanish language, to come to terms with the Martinez wealth and lifestyle, and to accept the things she couldn't change.

In a way, he'd been her mentor, and to now discover the shell of the man she'd once adored was heartbreaking.

At first she was tentative, unsure whether the affection they'd shared still existed. After all, it had been she who'd left under cover of night, leaving only a brief note for Marcello to find on his return home, and no word for anyone else.

'*Holà.*' It wasn't so much the greeting, but the husky-voiced delivery accompanied by a gentle smile that filled her eyes with unshed tears.

'Ramon.' She didn't hesitate in crossing to the cushioned chair where he sat. Nor did she pause in brushing her lips to his cheek. 'How are you?'

The dark eyes twinkled with humour. 'How do I look?'

She tilted her head slightly to one side. 'A little less the Martinez lion than I remember.'

'How beautifully you lie.' His soft laughter almost undid her. 'But I forgive you for indulging an old man.' He caught hold of her hand and held it within his own. 'Now introduce me to my great-granddaughter.'

Marcello moved forward with Nicki held in his arms.

'Nicki,' he said gently, 'this is Ramon.'

Ramon's features softened dramatically, and his eyes misted. 'Bring her closer.'

For a moment Nicki looked hesitant, then she nodded as Marcello offered a few soft, reassuring words.

'*Holà, Bisabuelo.*'

Shannay's eyes widened in startled surprise. The pronunciation was good. Who? Marcello...of course, possibly coached by Maria.

For a moment she had mixed feelings, then they were overcome by Ramon's obvious delight.

'Nicki. A beautiful name for a beautiful little girl,' he said gently.

'Marcello—my daddy—sometimes calls me *pequena*,' Nicki said solemnly. 'That means little.'

His smile melted Shannay's heart. 'Indeed it does. You must visit often, and I will teach you some Spanish.'

'I'll have to ask Mummy if it's OK.'

'Of course,' Ramon agreed with equal solemnity, and cast Shannay an enquiring glance.

'It will be a pleasure.' How could she say anything else?

'Marcello shall bring you.'

Nicki looked momentarily unsure. 'Mummy, too?'

'Naturally. We shall make it mornings, then you will have the rest of the day to explore.' He glanced up at the slight sound of a door opening. 'Ah, here is Sophia with our tea.'

Tea with delicious bite-size sandwiches and pastries, some pleasant conversation, after which Marcello indicated they should leave.

'*Hasta mañana.*'

Until tomorrow.

Carlo drove them past the Warner Bros Park, a visit to which Marcello promised as a treat in store.

'You're a busy man,' Shannay protested lightly.

'Impossible I have learnt to delegate?'

'Improbable.'

'You are wrong.'

She looked at him carefully. 'We don't expect you to give up your time.'

Dark eyes travelled to her mouth and lingered there a moment too long. 'It is my pleasure to do so.'

Pleasure being the operative word, and unmistakable.

Shannay could feel colour tinge her cheeks, and she shot him a dark glance before becoming seemingly engrossed in the scene beyond the car window.

It was during dinner that evening that she brought up his social life, and a firm reiteration she didn't require to be entertained…especially by him.

'Won't your—er—' she paused with deliberate delicacy '—current lover,' she lightly stressed, 'become impatient at your absence?'

One eyebrow slanted in silent mockery. 'From her bed?' And noted with interest the increased thud of a pulse at the base of her throat. 'Possibly,' he drawled, and took his time in adding, 'If I had one.'

She refused to rise to the bait. 'Estella has become the consummate mistress?'

'Something you would need to ask of her husband.'

Estella had married? 'I find it difficult to believe she gave up on you.'

His smile was a mere facsimile. 'It takes two, *amada,* and I was never a contender.'

It wasn't easy to feign indifference, but she managed it. 'Could we change the subject?'

'Yet you brought it up,' he reminded with hateful simplicity.

'Is Ramon in much pain?' She kept the faintly desperate edge from her voice, and had the impression it didn't fool him at all.

Marcello's gaze didn't shift from her own as he inclined his head. 'He has ongoing medical attention with a doctor and nurse in residence. It is his wish to remain at home.'

Shannay knew his condition, and the odds. There was little to be done, except keep him comfortable.

'I would ask that you and Nicki remain here until Ramon slips into a coma.'

She should have seen it coming, and she cursed herself for not foreseeing just this eventuality.

'I have a job,' she reminded. 'We have an agreement. After three weeks Nicki and I return to Perth.'

'I'm sure your leave can be extended on compassionate grounds.'

It could. If she wanted it extended.

The truth being she didn't trust herself to stay in Marcello's company any longer than she had to.

They shared a history, a potent chemistry she didn't dare stir into vibrant life.

He was dangerous, primitive, and intently focused.

A surge of helpless anger rose to the fore at his manipulation, and her gaze hardened as she sought a measure of control.

'You believe I brought you here with an ulterior motive in mind?'

How could she doubt it? *'Yes.'*

'Perhaps you'd care to elaborate?'

His voice was a silky drawl as his eyes pierced her own, silently daring her to avoid his gaze.

'I think you'll do whatever it takes to ensure you get what you want,' she retaliated heatedly.

'And what is it you imagine I want?'

'Nicki.'

His expression didn't change. 'Of course. What else?'

She couldn't bear to be in his presence a moment longer, and she stood to her feet, tossed aside her napkin and turned away from him.

'One day you won't run.'

Shannay swivelled and sent him a venomous glare. 'You *think?*'

He had the strong desire to haul her over his shoulder and carry her kicking and protesting to his bed.

As he had done once in the past, when mere words had

become an impossible means of communication. Kisses tempered by anger assumed reluctant passion, then became more, so much more, until there was no denial of need, or a mutual sensual recognition that overcame all else...until reality in the light of day intruded.

Was her memory of what they'd shared as hauntingly vivid as his own?

Did it keep her awake nights?

He was counting on it.

CHAPTER SEVEN

SHANNAY CHECKED her appearance, and wondered how she could look so calm, when her nerves were shot to pieces and it seemed as if a dozen butterflies were beating their wings madly inside her stomach.

She really didn't want to do this.

Re-entering the Madrid social scene had never been part of the plan.

Hell, *nothing* that had happened in the past few weeks formed part of any plan she could have envisaged in her worst nightmare!

Yet the evening represented a fundraiser for a worthy charity, one of a few supported by the Martinez corporation.

Marcello's attendance was a given and, as his purported newly reconciled wife, she was expected to appear by his side.

Something suitable to wear had been dealt with with remarkable ease. All it had taken was a phone call to a prominent boutique with her measurements to have a selection of gowns delivered to Marcello's home.

Now she viewed the *café-au-lait* gown in silk organza with its elegant, finely pleated bodice, thin spaghetti straps and full-length soft, flowing skirt, the stiletto-heeled evening shoes…and felt reasonably confident her choice was the right one.

Understated make-up with emphasis on her eyes, a faint

tinge of blush at her cheeks and lipgloss…with her hair in a smooth twist.

'You look like a princess.'

Shannay turned towards Nicki and blew her a kiss. 'Thank you.'

'*Gracias,*' her daughter corrected with a grin. 'Me and Maria are going to watch *Shrek.*'

'Just for a little while. When Maria says it's time for bed, you won't fuss. OK?'

''Kay.'

Time to go downstairs, join Marcello, then step into a Martinez chauffeured limousine…secure in the knowledge Nicki would be well looked after in Maria's care, with Carlo in charge, and a direct private line on speed-dial to both her and Marcello's cellphone.

Shannay collected the matching evening bag, then held out her hand. 'Come on, imp. Party-time.'

A faint knock on Nicki's bedroom door accompanied by the sound of a familiar male voice had the little girl racing through the connecting *en suite.*

'Daddy's here!'

Large as life and far too stunningly attractive in dark evening wear, Shannay perceived as she attempted without success to still the warmth flooding through her veins at the mere sight of him.

Fine white shirt linen provided a stark contrast with his olive skin and dark, well-groomed hair, his tailored suit displaying an impeccable fit as it moulded his superbly muscled frame.

It was little wonder women of all ages felt emboldened to flex their flirting skills in his presence, for he possessed a raw sexuality combined with the hint of something forbidden, almost verging on the savagely primitive.

A modern-day warrior who fought daily with powerful brokers in numerous countries around the world, constantly seeking an essential edge…and always watching his back.

Dark inscrutable eyes took in her slim form, the child regarding him with dancing anticipation, and he leant down and scooped Nicki into his arms.

'Isn't Mummy beautiful?' his daughter confided, and his mouth curved into a generous smile.

'Beautiful,' Marcello agreed. 'Just like you.'

A compliment that earned him an enthusiastic kiss to his cheek.

Ten minutes later Shannay sat in the rear seat of the limousine as it cleared the gates and traversed the avenue leading towards the main arterial route into the city.

'There's something missing,' Marcello drawled and reached into his jacket pocket, extracted a small velvet case and snapped it open.

'Give me your hand.'

He sensed her hesitation and simply caught hold of her left hand, and slid the exquisite baguette-style diamond ring onto the appropriate finger.

Her wedding ring. The one she'd left behind the night she'd fled his home, his country.

'I don't—'

'Want to wear it?' His dark eyes met hers and held them. 'But you will.'

'Why?'

'I would have thought it obvious.'

'The orchestrated reconciliation,' she acknowledged drily, and saw his cynical smile.

'Need I remind you the marriage remains intact?'

'For the time being.' She'd play the game for the duration of her stay, for Ramon's sake. An extra week or two was little to gift him from her lifetime.

The wide platinum diamond-encrusted band shot prisms of brilliantly coloured fire as the light caught the numerous facets, and its unaccustomed weight felt strange.

'There's also these.'

He revealed a pear-shaped diamond pendant and matching earrings he'd gifted her on their first wedding anniversary.

Without a word he leant towards her and attached the delicate platinum chain in place and fastened the clasp at her nape.

It took only seconds, but it felt like an age as his warm breath feathered her cheek, and the touch of his fingers at her nape wrought an intimacy in the close confines of the limousine.

How easy would it be to move her head a little and have her cheek brush his own? To turn into him and seek his mouth, feel the sensuous slide of his tongue in an erotic tasting that could never be enough…merely a tantalising preliminary to how the evening would end. As it had in the early days of their marriage.

A time when she had dared and teased, and exulted in every moment.

Now she sat still, waiting with indrawn breath for him to move away so her heartbeat could return to its normal rhythm.

She made a slightly strangled protest as he lifted his fingers to her ear and carefully attached the hooked pin of one ear-stud before tending to her other earlobe.

Shannay couldn't fault his touch, or accuse it lingered a little too long. But the action felt incredibly personal, intimate…and she had to fight against the way it affected her wayward emotions.

As he meant it to do?

And if so, to what purpose?

Physically, Marcello could do nothing to prevent her leaving the country.

So why this persistent niggle of doubt?

The hotel was one of the city's finest, and Shannay cursed Marcello afresh as she pinned a smile on her face and prepared to play an expected part.

Numerous photographers' cameras flashed as they alighted from the limousine and trod the red carpet into the foyer.

Marcello's hand was warm as it rested at the back of her waist, and the bodyguard who'd ridden up front in the limousine now flanked her as they moved towards the gracious staircase leading to the mezzanine level.

A well-remembered scene, Shannay perceived, with the beautiful people who mostly came to be seen. Women who chose to showcase designer gowns and expensive jewellery, gifted by husbands and lovers who presided as captains of industry.

Socialites, fashionistas, models…she caught a glimpse of a few familiar faces, smiled and kept her head high.

Waiters and waitresses dutifully presented trays of drinks, from which Marcello selected two flutes of champagne and placed one in her hand.

Alcohol on an empty stomach wasn't such a good idea, and she merely took a sip of the chilled bubbly liquid, then regarded the flute as a prop.

'Marcello!'

'Miguel and Shantal Rodriguez,' Marcello intoned quietly as a man and woman greeted them, followed by voluble Spanish…which Marcello immediately explained was not his wife's first language.

Shannay was supremely conscious of him at her side, the occasional touch of his hand at the edge of her waist, his attentive manner, and suppressed the wayward desire it was real, instead of the expected portrayal of a husband with his wife.

It was a relief when the large ballroom doors opened and guests were instructed to begin making their way to reserved seats at designated tables.

There was one face in the crowd Shannay subconsciously searched for, and failed to notice.

Estella de Cordova.

A woman whose presence at the evening's prestigious event would be obligatory.

Then there she was, tall, impossibly elegant in Versace only someone with a superb figure and an overdose of panache could wear.

Dark, thick, curling hair framed her perfect features, and an abundance of diamonds sparkled with every move she made.

The centre of attention as always, and actively seeking to make an impression.

Shannay's gaze shifted slightly to the man at her side. Distinguished, and at least fifteen years Estella's senior.

Estella de Cordova was known to scope out a room, hone in on her quarry, then patiently wait for the opportune moment to strike.

Somehow Shannay doubted anything had changed.

Impossible the news of Marcello's reconciliation with his Australian wife hadn't reached Estella's notice. Or the knowledge Shannay's attendance tonight at his side wouldn't garner speculation.

It wasn't so much a matter of if Estella would make her move, only when.

Not, she perceived, before the guests were all seated.

Those who had been aware of the purported affair between Estella de Cordova and Marcello Martinez would be subtly watching for the slightest sign to fuel the social gossip mill.

Shannay could almost sense it, and hated being the focus of speculative interest.

Sandro and Luisa moved into sight, and their exchanged greeting held politeness, faint smiles and a reassuring touch to Shannay's arm together with a whispered *"brava"* from Luisa a few seconds before they were shown to another table.

How…nice, Shannay conceded silently. A friendly ally.

The thought of calmly forking morsels of food into her mouth, sipping wine, and participating in meaningless conversation while waiting for Marcello's former mistress to strike was enough to ruin her appetite.

Maintaining a façade didn't help, for she was supremely conscious of her husband's presence, the faint, exclusive tones of his cologne and the essence of the man himself.

Worse, the tantalisation of having an intimate knowledge of his touch, the caress of his hands, his lips, the way he could make her body sigh, then heat with passion. The heights he helped her reach, and how he held her when she fell.

'It is good you have returned to Madrid.'

Shannay heard the heavily accented feminine voice, attached it to a woman seated directly opposite and offered a polite smile in acknowledgement.

'Thank you.'

'A man in your husband's position needs a wife by his side.'

But not a wife *and* a mistress.

And the mistress had won out.

Words she didn't care to voice. Didn't need to, surely? Estella's contretemps at the time had caused sufficient speculation.

'I'm sure Marcello didn't lack for a suitable companion.'

An understatement, if ever there was one. The women would have been lining up…keen, willing and able to serve in every way possible!

'Why—no. Marcello usually chose to accompany his aunt, or appear alone.'

He did? How…surprising, was the only word that came to mind.

Shannay took a sip of wine, then followed it with a measure of water, and became aware of Marcello's interested gaze.

'The food isn't to your liking?'

'It's fine,' she hastened quickly. 'I'm not that hungry.'

His eyes held hers, and saw more than she wanted him to see. Without a word he speared a morsel of food from his plate and offered it to her. 'Try this. You'll enjoy it.'

Don't, she silently pleaded, and veiled her eyes against the deliberate sensuality evident.

It's a game, she reminded. We're like players on a stage, acting out an anticipated part.

With care, she cupped his hand, drew the proffered fork to her lips and eased the morsel into her mouth.

Her lashes swept up to reveal a provocative gleam as she edged the tip of her tongue to the corner of her mouth, let it slide fractionally over her lower lip, then carefully bit the morsel of food without taking her eyes from his own.

And watched his eyes darken.

Mission accomplished.

Shannay offered a faint smile in silent compliment to his acting ability, then momentarily froze as he slid a hand to her nape and gently massaged the knot of tension there.

To anyone viewing the subtle actions they would appear as two lovers who could barely wait to get a room.

Was that what he wanted to convey?

To many…or just Estella?

Shannay waited a few minutes, then she leaned towards him. 'You're verging on overkill, *querido*,' she warned in a softly taunting voice.

Marcello lowered his head to hers. 'There's the need to set a precedent.'

She took the opportunity to surreptitiously check her cellphone, saw an SMS message alerting Nicki had gone to sleep at eight-thirty, and felt a sense of relief.

There were speeches in between numerous courses, some discourses brief and amusing…others long as the charity was lauded, together with the efforts of the tireless volunteers without whose help the fundraiser would not have been as successful.

Or at least that was the overall drift, and she joined in the applause, aware Marcello had placed his arm across the back of her chair.

An action which brought him close, and heightened her level of awareness.

As he meant it to do?

Did he know the effect he had on her?

She assured herself she didn't like or condone what he was doing. Or his manipulation. For at almost every turn she was caught in a trap, bound by love for her daughter, her affection for an elderly ill man, and now the subterfuge of deception.

Only for a certain length of time, she reminded, for her sojourn in Madrid would reach an end and she'd return with Nicki to resume their life in Perth.

Custody arrangements involving travel would be minimal for the next two years, and Marcello's visits brief, if relatively frequent.

She could cope. So too would Nicki.

So what if she played the game according to Marcello's dictum in the presence of others?

It was only temporary.

At that moment there was an entertainment announcement, and a female singer offered a rousing rendition in Spanish while colourfully attired back-up dancers performed an energetic routine.

Coffee was served, and Shannay declined the strong espresso in favour of tea.

It was the time of evening when guests were no longer restricted to their seats, and several rose to seek out friends, to linger, share coffee and conversation.

Would Estella make her move now? Or engineer a staged encounter as Marcello rose to leave?

She told herself she didn't care. But she did, and a tension headache took hold behind her eyes.

Presenting a sparkling façade had taken its toll. So too had attempting to correlate much of a language she hadn't practised in a few years.

Consequently it was a relief when Marcello withdrew his cellphone and summoned their driver to wait out front.

There was the opportunity for a few brief words with Sandro and Luisa before their attention was diverted.

They were about to exit the ballroom minutes later when a familiar sultry feminine voice purred a greeting, and a sinking feeling manifested itself in the pit of her stomach.

'Estella.' She could do polite. It really was the only way to go.

Was it chance or design the man at Estella's side drew Marcello into conversation, conveniently allowing Estella an opportunity to deliver a verbal barb or three?

'I see Marcello was able to persuade you to return.' There

was a very subtle pause. 'Not very clever of you to deny him the child.' Her smile failed to reach the coolness in her eyes. 'I doubt he'll forgive you for that.'

If the figurative knives were out, it was time to dispense with the niceties. 'You don't read the media news?'

'The reconciliation announcement?' A soft, humourless laugh escaped her lips. 'A mere ploy to soothe Ramon's rapidly ailing health.'

'And this concerns you…because?'

Something shifted in the woman's eyes. 'He's a very—' Estella paused, weighting the momentary silence with innuendo '—special man.'

'Yes, he is.' Shannay aimed for a secretive smile, and saw Estella's mouth tighten a little.

'If you'll excuse us?' Marcello's voice held a silky quality Estella chose to heed.

'Of course.'

It could have been worse, Shannay accorded as the limousine eased its way clear of the hotel's entrance and joined the flow of traffic.

She let her eyelids drift down in an attempt to shut out the neon lights and the frequent stab of headlights as the headache moved towards migraine territory.

'You don't have your medication with you?'

He knew? 'If I did, I'd have taken some by now.'

There was the faint whisper of sound, followed by another as he released both safety belts, then firm hands positioned her to rest against him. A male arm curved down her back and settled over her thigh, holding her there as she began to protest.

'Just close your eyes and relax.'

Relax? With her body curled into the contours of his, her

head cradled against the curve of his shoulder? Her face mere inches from his own?

He had to be joking!

Warmth heated her veins, tantalising her senses as the perceived intimacy invaded pleasure places they had no right to be.

It wasn't what she wanted. And knew her mind to be at odds with the dictates of her body.

How easy would it be to slip free a few buttons on his shirt and slide her hand to rest against the strong beat of his heart. To feel it kick into a quickened beat as she caressed a male nipple.

Hear his husky murmur as she lowered her hand and traced the hardened outline of his arousal held in tight restraint within the confines of his evening trousers.

To tease a little, then lift her mouth and savour the touch of his in a preliminary to what they'd soon share in the privacy of their bedroom.

A slow, teasing discovery, or a quick shedding of clothes as desire and need meshed and became electrifying passion.

A time when they'd been in perfect sync, two halves of a whole…and she'd innocently believed nothing and no one could touch them.

How wrong had she been.

It almost made her wish it were possible to turn back the clock, and possess the power to change actions and words.

Except it was done, and the past couldn't be altered.

Did Marcello have any regrets?

How could he?

He hadn't followed her to Perth.

Hadn't sought to make contact.

As far as he was concerned, she could have vanished from the face of the earth.

Until a chance encounter had brought her beneath his radar.

Because of Nicki.

Let's not be fooled in thinking otherwise.

So what in hell was she doing resting against him like this? Savouring a little self-indulgence?

It would be simple to push against him and straighten into a sitting position...except his arms tightened and held her in place.

'Stay there. We're almost home.'

All the more reason for her to move.

This time he didn't try to stop her.

Nor did he attempt to touch her as they alighted from the limousine and moved indoors.

He merely acknowledged her "goodnight" with a brief nod, and watched as she ascended the stairs.

CHAPTER EIGHT

'Is RAMON GOING to die?'

The plaintive query from so young a child was heart-rending, and Shannay went down on one knee and gathered her daughter close.

'He's very sick,' she said gently.

'Like Fred.'

Fred had been a pet white mouse who'd developed a tumour, and been replaced, after due ceremony, by a goldfish.

'Like Fred,' she agreed solemnly.

'It'll be sad,' Nicki ventured, and Shannay inclined her head, then sought to offer a distraction by suggesting a swim in the pool.

It was a warm day, with no breeze to riffle the tree-leaves, and together they donned swimsuits, lathered on sunscreen cream, then gathered up towels, alerted Carlo as to their whereabouts, and wandered down to the pool.

Nicki was like a fish in water, diving, floating, and showing her swimming prowess with a credible crawl...for a young child.

It was fun to play, to splash, laugh a little and temporarily relax her guard.

'Daddy!'

Shannay turned slowly in the direction Nicki indicated, and

saw Marcello's tall masculine figure walking the path through the grounds towards the few marble steps leading to the pool and its surrounds.

Attired as he was in a short black towelling robe with a towel slung over one shoulder, his intention to join them was obvious, and she tried to ignore the unbidden convulsing sensation deep inside.

She didn't want to feel like this, and hated her body's traitorous reaction. It wasn't fair to be constantly reminded of the sensual heat that coursed through her veins in remembered passion.

With every passing day it became more intense, the memories disruptive. The nights were worse when she lay alone in her bed, so aware of his presence as he slept in a suite not far from her own.

Did he sleep easily, or did he lie awake as she did, caught up in emotional hunger?

Enough, a silent voice taunted.

Yet being here, in his home and his constant company, attacked her defences and seriously eroded them.

There was a part of her that wished he absented himself in the city each day, instead of utilising the benefits of modern technology to keep in touch with the business world from home.

Although she had to accept he had reason enough to rearrange his life in order to spend as much time as possible with his daughter.

Now here he was, about to shrug off a robe and join them in the water.

Wearing, Shannay noted with a quick glance, a very respectable pair of black boxer swim shorts.

Her heart rate accelerated at the sight of his powerful frame with its fluid flex of muscle and sinew, and his eyes caught hers for a few timeless seconds before she deliberately shifted her attention to Nicki.

'Daddy, watch me swim.'

He did, slipping into the water and applauding his daughter's efforts as Nicki went through her paces.

Shannay was conscious of the brevity of her *maillot*, cut high at the hip and a halter-neck plunging to a deep V between breasts a little fuller since Nicki's birth.

Had he noticed?

Oh, for heaven's sake...*stop*, she cautioned in silent castigation. What are you *thinking?*

Yet the warmth of his touch as he'd cradled her close in the limousine had stirred something deep inside, reminding her too vividly of everything they'd shared...and never would again.

So get over it.

'Nicki is a beautiful child,' Marcello opined quietly. 'Obedient and unspoilt. You've done well with her.'

She looked at him carefully. 'A compliment, Marcello?'

'Is it so difficult to accept I might offer you one?'

He was close, within touching distance, and she stilled the almost irresistible urge to move away.

'In the circumstances, yes,' she stated coolly, and heard a faint drawling quality enter his voice.

'Perhaps it is wise to ignore circumstances.' His pause held a weight of meaning she chose not to explore. 'And attempt to move on.'

'I was doing fine,' Shannay offered sweetly. 'Until you dragged me here under threat.' With that, she used breaststroke to glide effortlessly away and did her best to ignore him.

Difficult, when Nicki sought his attention at every turn, laughing with delight as he splashed her, then allowed her to catch him.

He was good with her. Kind, playful and clearly her idol.

Daddy peppered her conversation with tremendous regularity, and she squealed as he lifted her onto his shoulders and ascended the tiled steps leading out from the pool.

Maria served tea in the *sala,* together with a nutritious evening meal for Nicki, whose bedtime was gradually being extended to conform with local custom.

Where Shannay predicted difficulties, none appeared to exist. Nicki had slipped happily into her new lifestyle, accepting the changes with surprising ease.

Instead *she* was the one having problems as ambivalent emotions invaded her being, causing increasing turmoil with every passing day.

'Mummy's turn tonight,' Nicki declared as Shannay tucked her into bed and picked up a book of fairy tales, aware Marcello had taken a chair close by.

It was hard to shut him out as she endeavoured to focus on reading the story of the princess and the pea.

He was *there,* a physical entity impossible to ignore, and she was conscious of his hooded gaze, the sheer dynamic presence of the man.

Nicki listened with rapt attention, valiantly fighting sleep until her eyelids drifted down and her breathing settled into a slow even rhythm.

Shannay carefully closed the book, checked the bedcovers, the monitor and night-light, then she paused in the doorway before closing the door softly behind her.

Marcello followed, and she turned at the same time he did and brushed against him.

An automatic apology fell from her lips, and she moved quickly to widen the distance between them as they both traversed the gallery leading to the staircase.

'Nicki is fortunate to have you as a mother.'

A flippant response rose in her throat, and didn't find voice. Instead she uttered a quiet, 'I can't imagine my life without her.'

Dark eyes swept her features as they began descending the stairs. 'There is a solution.'

Something took hold of her emotions and turned them upside down. 'Such as?' She paused as they reached the spacious foyer.

'Stay.'

Shannay closed her eyes, then opened them again. 'With you? I don't think so.'

'It's a large house. You would have an enviable lifestyle. And never need to be parted from Nicki,' he added.

Shannay was suddenly icily calm. 'Define *enviable?*'

'An unlimited expense account. Jewellery. Any vehicle you care to name. A personal bodyguard. Everything the wife of a very wealthy man can provide.'

She wanted to hit him. 'You think I *care* about a collection of designer gowns, the Manolo Blahniks and Jimmy Choos, jewellery?' She paused for breath. 'Attending the opera, the theatre, charity fundraisers in all their various guises, glittering first nights, that parties are my ultimate choice in entertainment?' She was filled with pent-up anger, and unable to prevent it from spilling over. 'Live in this mansion, give my time to charity committees and become the exemplary wife in and out of the bedroom? You think any of that is important to me?'

Marcello regarded her with a degree of amusement. 'Not even the bedroom?'

'No.' And knew she lied.

His voice became dangerously soft. 'Then, perhaps you'd care to elaborate?'

She tilted her chin a little and seared his dark eyes with her own. If only it were possible to turn back the clock, to recapture the love they'd once shared. Except that didn't form part of any equation she could envisage.

'You think you can buy whatever you want. Everything has a price. Even me. You're so wrong!' Her eyes assumed a molten hue.

'As to your suggestion…' She was almost beyond words. 'Forget it!'

She took a deep breath to help control her rising disbelief. 'Not even for Nicki's sake will I be trapped in a loveless marriage,' she added with pent-up vehemence.

An eyebrow rose in mocking silence at her lack of hesitation.

'You broke my heart once.' Any hope it had healed went out the window the moment she heard his voice and saw his image on video camera as he stood in the entrance bay of her apartment building just a few weeks ago. 'No way will I give you the chance to do it again.'

'I see I didn't make myself clear,' Marcello drawled. 'We not only share the same roof, we occupy the same room, the same bed.'

'Let me get this right. You're offering sex as a bonus?'

A muscle bunched at the edge of his jaw. 'A normal marriage. The possibility of adding to our family.'

'Forgive me.' She was on a roll, and like a runaway train she couldn't stop. 'I've experienced your version of *normal*, and I hated the way it worked out.'

'And nothing I say will convince you otherwise?'

Shannay drew herself up to her full height and glared at him with a look that would have seared a lesser man to a crisp. 'No.' With that she turned on her heel and began retracing her steps.

The thought of sitting opposite him calmly forking food into her mouth didn't appeal. Besides, she wasn't hungry.

Instead, she'd retrieve a book, go settle somewhere and read.

It would have been a good plan if she'd been able to concentrate on the written word.

After a while she tossed the book aside and turned on the television, only to channel-hop in a bid to find something of interest.

A cooking programme looked good, although it only served to remind her that she'd deliberately missed dinner.

OK, so admit you're mad at him.

To think of agreeing to his so-called proposal is an insult.

It hadn't been his wealth and position that had attracted her to him in the first place. Dammit, she hadn't even known who he was!

The next few weeks couldn't pass quickly enough, then she'd return *home* with Nicki and resume an ordinary life.

She must have slept, for she came sharply awake at the sound of a child's cry, followed by a heart-wrenching sobbing.

Ohmigod...*Nicki.*

Shannay raced through the connecting *en suite* to find Nicki sitting up in bed drenched in tears, and she scooped her onto her lap and held her close.

'Sweetheart, what's wrong?'

The words had barely emerged from her mouth when Marcello entered the room, crossed to her side and queried quietly,

'A bad dream?'

Concern shadowed her features. 'She's never woken like this before.' She pressed a cheek to Nicki's temple. 'Tell Mummy, darling.'

Gradually the sobs reduced to intermittent hiccups, and Shannay was hardly aware of Marcello's absence until he pressed a damp face-washer into her hand, which she proceeded to use.

'There,' she murmured gently. 'That's better.'

Marcello hunkered down and took hold of his daughter's hand, only to mask his feelings as Nicki looked at him with large sorrow-filled eyes.

'I don't want Bisabuelo Ramon to die like Fred.'

He spared Shannay a quick, enquiring glance, then smoothed a hand over Nicki's head on hearing the brief explanation. 'Sometimes when people and animals are very very sick and medicine can no longer help them get better, they go to a special place where they're no longer in pain.'

'Like Fred.'

His smile held gentle warmth. 'Yes, just like Fred,' he agreed softly.

'I talked to Fred all the time when he was sick.'

'As you do when we visit Ramon, *si?*'

An earnest look entered her childish features and pierced his heart. 'Can we see him tomorrow?'

'Of course.'

'Every day?'

'Every day, I promise.'

'I like him a lot.'

'And he loves you very much.'

Nicki turned her head and looked at her mother. 'I think I'll go back to sleep now.'

The simplistic logic of children, Shannay perceived as she preceded Marcello out onto the gallery and quietly closed the door behind her.

He was close…too close, and she was conscious of the black T-shirt moulding his muscular frame, the jeans he'd quickly dragged on at the sound of Nicki's first cry.

Did he still sleep naked between the sheets?

Shannay tried to ignore the image that rose too readily to mind…and failed miserably.

How was it possible to crave the touch of a man she professed to hate?

It didn't make sense to be so *drawn,* to want to lean in against him, lift her mouth to his and savour all he chose to gift her.

Marcello caught the darkness in her eyes, the way her lower lip trembled a little…and lowered his head to her own, tasting the sweetness that was hers alone, heard the soft sigh whisper in her throat, and chose a gentle exploration that teased and tantalised, until she reached for him, holding his head fast as she angled her mouth into his own.

It felt good. *He* felt so good. The way his hands slid over her shoulders to rest at her waist as he drew her slender frame in against him, and she sensed his hunger, knew it met and matched her own.

His mouth became flagrantly sensual, deepening with devastating effect as he swept her steadily beyond rational thought to a place where nothing else mattered…except the need for more, so much *more.*

The long oversized T-shirt she wore proved no barrier to his questing hands as they sought the hemline and settled on silken flesh.

One hand cupped her bottom while the other slid to caress her breast, shaping the soft fullness as he brushed a thumb back and forth across the tender peak, feeling it swell and harden beneath his touch.

He eased his mouth free from her own and traced a path down the arched line of her throat to settle in the hollow at its base, before seeking the sensitive curve at the edge of her neck.

An open-mouthed kiss there sent a shivery sensation arching through her body, and her fingers sought and freed the snap fastening of his jeans in the need to explore warm muscle and sinew.

With one quick movement she tugged his T-shirt high and slid tactile fingers over the hard musculature beneath his ribcage, then slipped to trace his navel, before easing low over his arousal to cup his scrotum…and squeeze a little.

A husky growl sounded close to her ear, and strong hands slid beneath her knees as he carried her down to the master suite and used the heel of one foot to close the door before easing her down the hard length of his body to her feet.

Feverish hands rapidly dispensed with what clothes remained, and Shannay uttered a sharp cry as Marcello lifted her high and wrapped her thighs round his waist before lowering his mouth to her breast.

Sensation radiated from her central core, and she gasped out loud as he took the tender peak between his teeth and rolled it gently, taking her from intense pleasure almost to the edge of pain.

It was she who sought the curve at the edge of his neck…and suckled there, deliberately marking him before soothing the bite with the tip of her tongue.

He shifted slightly, and slowly lowered the most vulnerable and sensitive part of her anatomy over his swollen arousal, held her there, then gently rocked her until she groaned out loud in frustration.

'Now.' It was a muttered agonised plea he refused to heed, and she dug her fingers in his hair and tugged a little.

'Please.'

In one smooth movement he slid her down and onto him, then inch by tortuous inch until he filled her.

Oh, dear heaven, it felt so good. Joined with him, awash with coalescing sensation as passion escalated and demanded more.

It was then he moved to the bed and carefully eased her down onto the sheets, and she tossed her head in abject denial as he withdrew, then began a tracery of feather-light kisses over each breast in turn, pausing to savour there before moving lower over her abdomen.

She wanted his mouth on hers…except he had a different destination in mind, and she cried out as he sought the moist heat, laving the clitoris into vibrant, erotic life, sending her high with sensual spasms so intense she cried out as each wave consumed her body and reached right down to her soul.

Then, and only then did he enter her again, surging to the hilt in one powerful thrust, and she became boneless, so caught up with witching abandon she no longer knew who she was…only aware she never wanted this shameless rapture to end as she arched her body and took him again and again until they reached the brink, then soared together in glorious ecstasy.

It took a while for her rapid breathing to slow and return to something resembling normal, and she held on as he carefully rolled onto his back and took her with him, cradling her close, his lips buried against her temple.

It was then he felt the moistness on her cheek, and he smoothed a gentle hand over her hair, tucking some of it behind her ear as he searched her tear-filled eyes.

'I hurt you?'

She didn't trust herself to speak, and she simply shook her head.

He lifted a hand and brushed her cheek with his thumb, then he caressed her lips with his own, softly and with such tenderness fresh tears spilled and ran down each cheek in warm rivulets to pause at the edges of her mouth.

Light fingers traced her spine, soothing her as she buried her face into the curve of his neck.

She didn't want to move. Didn't feel as if she *could*.

Soon, she silently vowed, she'd disentangle herself from his arms, catch up her abandoned T-shirt, then quietly retreat to her room.

But for now she'd simply enjoy the aftermath of good sex. Very good sex, she amended silently, and felt the faint pull of unused muscles, the sheer euphoria of sensual fulfilment.

There was a part of her which yearned to be held through the night, to be comforted by the beat of Marcello's heart beneath her hand, her cheek. To move in the night and be gathered in close against him.

She must have dozed, for she drifted awake to the realisation of a warm body curved round her own, a steady heartbeat against her back...and memory surfaced in a slow, unfolding image.

No. It was a dream, surely? Like one of many which haunted her mind in the dark hours of night.

Yet this was no dream. The arms which held her were real. And she froze for a few interminable seconds, then carefully, slowly, she began to ease herself free. Only to feel those arms tighten as warm breath teased her hair.

'You're not going anywhere.'

'Please.' Her voice was a strangled whisper of sound, and she felt the press of his mouth against her nape.

'What if—?'

'Nicki?'

Ohmigod, *Nicki*. What was she thinking?

Be honest, a wicked voice taunted. You weren't *thinking* at all. 'If she wakes and I'm not there.' The words tumbled out in a rush, only to come to a halt as Marcello pressed a hand over her mouth.

'Don't,' he cautioned quietly as he cupped her face and

kissed her, slowly, lingeringly, as he felt his body harden with need and her own response.

With care he gathered her in, his persuasive touch wreaking havoc with her emotions as he branded her his own in a highly sensitised coupling that surpassed what they'd previously shared.

CHAPTER NINE

SHANNAY WOKE to the muted sound of the shower running, registered the large bed, the rumpled sheets…and closed her eyes in automatic reflex as memory provided a vivid image of what had transpired through the night and with whom.

If there was the slightest edge of doubt, her body bore numerous signs to disprove it. Not the least of which was the need to shower and retreat to her room to dress.

Nicki.

She reached out and checked her discarded watch, then let out her indrawn breath. Six. It was only six o'clock. Nicki rarely stirred before seven.

The shower ceased, and she hurriedly tossed back the covers and slid from the bed.

Where was her T-shirt? A hasty glance over the floor revealed nothing. Had Marcello picked it up?

Oh, hell, surely not Maria? At this early hour, the likelihood was so remote it was immediately dismissed.

So where the devil was it? She required *something* to cover her nudity, and she crossed to Marcello's walk-in wardrobe, selected the first shirt her fingers touched, slid an arm into each sleeve, then re-emerged into the bedroom at the same time Marcello emerged from the *en suite* with a towel hitched at his hips.

Broad shoulders, expanse of naked chest, the fluid flex of muscle as he towelled his hair dry, powerful thighs.

There was no chance she could escape before he saw her, and almost as if he sensed her presence he lowered his arms.

A slow smile curved his generous mouth as he caught her drinking in the sight of him, and his lips curved as her gaze slithered to a point near the vicinity of his left shoulder.

'*Buenos dias.*' His voice was a husky, intimate drawl as he crossed to stand within touching distance, and she was powerless to prevent the descent of his head as he covered her mouth with his own in a slow, evocative kiss.

Her eyes dilated with a conflicting mix of emotions as he lifted his mouth fractionally from her own, and he had no trouble determining each and every one of them.

'Marcello—'

He cut off the tumble of words by the simple expediency of brushing his lips over hers…and sensed rather than heard her soft moan in protest as it remained locked in her throat.

Her eyelids drifted down, only to spring open again seconds later as his hand cupped her breast and teased the tender peak before slipping down over her abdomen to the soft curls at the apex of her thighs.

His touch was incredibly gentle as he stroked the sensitive bud still acutely responsive from his attention, and he absorbed the slight hitch in her breath as he sent her spiralling to climax, then he held her until the spasms diminished.

For a moment the past didn't exist as he brushed his lips to each closed eyelid in turn before releasing her.

'Great fashion accessory, *mi mujer.*' He ran a finger down

the shirt's open edge, his gleaming gaze locking with hers. 'Although I prefer you without it.'

Shannay dragged the edges together in a delayed sense of modesty as she turned away from him.

He waited until she reached the door, then cautioned quietly, 'From now on you sleep here with me.'

She didn't answer, for she was unable to find the words in acquiescence or argument as she turned the door-handle and walked from the room.

It was a relief to discover Nicki still fast asleep, and she quickly showered, then dressed in a gypsy-style skirt in shades of brown and a fashionable top, dried her hair, caught it in a casual twist and anchored it with a wide hinged clip, added lipgloss, then heard her daughter begin to stir.

Breakfast was a convivial meal eaten out on the glass-enclosed terrace, and Shannay endeavoured to focus on Nicki's excited conversation with Marcello on learning they were to experience the Aquopolis theme park after their morning visit with Ramon.

Something she achieved with difficulty, given the distraction provided by Marcello's presence directly opposite.

If she looked at him, her eyes betrayed her as they settled briefly on his mouth, and recalled vividly its erotic tasting. How his hands had explored her body and gifted untold pleasure. And, ultimately, the sex.

Mind-blowing electrifying passion that liquefied her bones and made her *his* more thoroughly than any words he might offer.

It shouldn't have happened.

She should have done more than utter a weak-willed protest, then given in to the provocative power of his touch and its pagan promise to banish her restraint.

Worse, allow him to lead her through intoxicating desire to join him again and again in mesmeric primitive climax.

His possession had made her acutely aware of sensitive tissues, and she could still feel the slight throb deep within resulting from his sexual presence.

It was…entrancing, consuming, and made her supremely conscious of what they'd shared. And would again.

Unless she chose to deny him.

Except denying him meant also denying herself, and she hated the disruptive annihilating *need* he generated in her with such ease.

'Mummy, you're not listening.'

Shannay summoned a smile and avoided meeting Marcello's gaze as she gave Nicki her whole attention.

She knew what he would see, and she refused to allow him the benefit of reading her mind, for he managed to divine her innermost thoughts despite her efforts to the contrary.

'We need to pack swimming gear for the visit to Aquopolis?' She hazarded the guess, and heard his faint chuckle at Nicki's audible sigh.

'Daddy says we can take a picnic to another park. Not tomorrow, but the day after.'

'That sounds lovely, darling.' She noticed her daughter's empty cereal bowl. 'What would you like on your toast?'

A return to the prosaic might have fooled Nicki, but she doubted the man seated opposite was under any such illusion, and it was a relief to temporarily escape when the meal concluded.

Ramon appeared to have faded slightly, his air of fragility a little more pronounced, yet his smile was warm and his eyes displayed delight as Nicki greeted him with affection.

Their visit was brief, on medical advice, for he seemed to tire more easily with each passing day.

Aquopolis proved to be a wonderful attraction, with plenty of fun to keep Nicki enthralled for several hours, for there were slides and numerous water features. Add a picnic lunch, and their daughter pronounced it *heaven*.

It was late when they left, and Nicki barely made it through her bath and a light evening meal before falling asleep within seconds of her head touching the pillow.

Shannay retreated to her suite to shower and change for dinner…only to discover her clothes reposing in the capacious wardrobe were no longer there.

The few drawers into which she'd stowed some personal items were now empty, and when she examined the adjoining *en suite,* all of her toiletries and make-up had been removed.

Marcello?

Or Maria, acting on his instructions?

Whatever…transferring her and her belongings to the master suite wasn't going to happen.

One night's transgression was enough.

There wasn't going to be a repeat.

With that in mind, she walked the gallery to his suite and entered without bothering to knock.

The shower was running, and she quickly crossed to the second walk-in wardrobe, retrieved her clothing and tossed it onto the bed, then she gathered up her personal items and transferred them to her room further along the gallery before returning to clear what remained.

Drawers she'd utilised in the past held everything she needed, and she was in the process of scooping them out when a deep, drawling voice momentarily arrested the movement of her hands.

'Looking for something?'

She took a few seconds to draw a deep breath, then she turned to face him, hating the sudden traitorous curl unfurling deep inside at the sight of his near-naked frame.

'I'm not moving into your room.'

Marcello slanted an eyebrow. 'You'd prefer me to move into yours?'

Shannay wasn't deceived by his even tone. 'No.'

'Then we have a problem.'

'No, we don't.'

'You intend to slink in here in the dead of night and leave at dawn?'

She tilted her chin and sent him a steady look. 'Last night was—'

'An aberration? A mistake?' The dangerous silkiness in his voice took hold of her nerve-ends and tugged a little.

'We each became carried away and indulged ourselves with sex?'

A sudden lump rose in her throat, and she attempted to swallow it in order to speak. 'Yes.'

'Justify the night however you choose. It doesn't change where you'll sleep.'

He watched the colour leave her cheeks, and hardened his heart. 'The bed's large, and sex,' he gave the word a faint emphasis, 'won't be on the menu unless you choose for it to be.'

Share the same bed, lie within touching distance… 'You have to be joking!'

'No.' He turned and moved towards his walk-in wardrobe. 'I'm going to dress for dinner.' He paused fractionally.

'Transfer everything to your room, if that's what you want. But if you go to bed there, you'll wake up in mine.'

Shannay merely glared at him and marched into the *en suite,* where she stripped off her clothes and took a long, hot shower in the hope it might help diminish her anger.

OK, so it was war, she declared silently as she dried off with a towel, then she wound it sarong-style around her body, secured it above her breasts and re-entered the bedroom.

Marcello caught the heat of battle apparent, and veiled his eyes against a faint gleam of humour as he rolled back his shirt-cuffs, then slid his feet into comfortable leather loafers.

'Did anyone tell you you're *impossible?*'

He had the satisfaction of offering—'*Touché.*'

She bore the look of someone much younger than her years with unbrushed hair and features free of make-up.

He restrained the desire to cross the room, dispense with the towel and kiss her senseless.

The fact he *could* provided a degree of satisfaction.

'Maria has dinner waiting.'

Shannay almost told him precisely what he could do with dinner, except she didn't trust herself to speak. Instead she extracted fresh underwear from a drawer, caught up a dress, then disappeared into the *en suite* again.

In an act of defiance she took longer than necessary, and emerged to discover he was conversing in French on his cell-phone.

She selected a pair of heeled sandals and secured the straps.

'Problems?' she queried sweetly as he closed the connection.

'Nothing I can't handle.'

'How…eminently satisfying to be the epitome of professionalism.'

He almost laughed, for she was unlike any woman he knew. 'Shall we adjourn downstairs?'

'Oh, by all means, let's adjourn.'

Sassy, definitely sassy. He wondered if she'd be quite so brave when they returned upstairs to retire for the night.

Maria had excelled herself, providing a rice pilaf to die for, a fresh salad, with a fruit flan for dessert.

'I'd like to take Nicki into the city tomorrow afternoon,' Shannay declared as she poured coffee, and made tea for herself.

'A shop-till-you-drop mission?'

She shook her head. 'Some small gifts to take home for a few of her friends. Something special for Anna.'

'On the condition both Carlo and I accompany you.'

'We could take the metro.'

'No.'

'A limousine and a bodyguard?' she queried with intentional mockery, and met his studied gaze.

'A necessary precaution.'

The Martinez billions were tied up in numerous corporations throughout the world. It was a given Marcello's personal fortune had escalated dramatically over the past four years.

So many assets. Yet only a few knew the extent of the Martinez benevolence to various charities, the hospitals they'd funded in third world countries.

It made the family a target. At risk from the insurgents who hated wealth and all it represented. The beautiful people who appeared to have everything while the less fortunate lived in tenements and fought for food.

During the two years of her marriage she'd given tirelessly of her time to help Penè organise events for charity, frequently suffering the older woman's acerbic tongue and endless criticism as they worked together.

Possibly Ramon's daughter saw it as a necessity to figuratively strengthen the spine of her nephew's wife, and her manner had achieved that, not without some resentment and restrained anger on Shannay's part at the time.

'If you insist,' Shannay conceded, aware that to argue with him over the protection issue was a waste of time. 'On the condition you allow me to judge what purchases are bought. I won't have Nicki acquire an inflated sense of her own importance and become a spoilt little madam.'

Marcello inclined his head. 'We'll drive into the city after visiting with Ramon.'

'Thank you.'

She finished her tea, then she transferred everything from the table onto a mobile trolley and wheeled it into the kitchen. It took only minutes to stow food into the refrigerator and stack the dishwasher.

'I need to make a few international calls, send some emails,' Marcello informed as she returned to the dining room.

Good. With luck she'd be asleep in her room by the time he came upstairs.

As a plan, it worked very well. Except she failed to take into consideration he'd carry through with his threat.

For she came sharply awake as her room was flooded with light, followed seconds later by firm hands lifting her effortlessly against a hard male chest as Marcello calmly carried her along the gallery to the master suite.

'You fiend.' The accusation came out as a strangled whisper as she clenched a fist and thumped it against his shoulder.

An action which had no effect whatsoever, and she angled her head, then sank her teeth into hard muscle, heard his indrawn breath and then yelped as he closed the door behind him with one hand and released her to stand on the floor.

'Get into bed.' His voice was a silken drawl. 'And shut that sassy mouth, before I'm tempted to shut it for you.'

She cast him a furious look that should have withered him on the spot. 'Go to hell.'

Without a further word he hefted her over one shoulder and crossed to the bed, then he slid between the covers, placed her struggling body firmly to one side and curved his own around her.

A simple movement and the light was extinguished, and she lay there fuming, desperately wanting to fight, but aware precisely what it would lead to if she did.

'Go to sleep.'

Sure. That was likely!

Held close against him, absorbing his body heat, and attempting to ignore the intense sensuality apparent?

As if *sleep* was going to happen any time soon!

Yet the day's events coupled with the previous night finally caught up with her, and the last thing she remembered was feeling…safe.

Once again Shannay woke to find herself alone in the large bed, and she had a moment of displacement before realisation hit.

It was morning, she'd apparently slept through the night without waking, curled against the man she'd sworn not to be with…and the knowledge he'd won out raised her anger levels an extra notch or two.

Yet sleep was the operative word, for they hadn't…had they?

Of course not. Sex with Marcello wasn't something she had to think twice to recall!

The fact Marcello had kept his word rankled slightly. So too did the fact he'd held her close through the night and made no attempt to seduce her into awareness.

If he had, she would, she assured as she traversed the gallery to her room, have fought him tooth and nail.

So why this vague feeling of disappointment?

It didn't make sense.

She checked on Nicki, saw she was still asleep, and quickly tended to her usual early-morning routine, then she dressed in a skirt and knit-top. By which time Nicki was awake.

Marcello was nowhere in sight when they went downstairs to breakfast, and he joined them with an apology as she was in the process of helping Nicki peel back the shell of her boiled egg.

With childish happiness Nicki lifted her face to accept the brush of his lips to her cheek, and returned the favour.

Shannay felt her eyes widen as he crossed to her side and bestowed a similar salutation…unusual in their daughter's presence, and one which garnered her surprise.

What was he playing at?

A discussion regarding plans on the day's agenda saw them through breakfast, and there was time for Nicki to develop her swimming skills before drying off and retreating upstairs to change.

Lunch was a leisurely meal eaten out on the covered terrace, followed by a siesta.

There was a part of her that wanted to play tourist, to wander at will, pause at a café for refreshments and hunt for bargains.

Except with Marcello and Carlo in attendance, playing tourist wasn't going to happen.

They'd agreed to meet in the foyer at four, visit Ramon, then head into the city.

She chose a black tailored straight skirt and white blouse, added minimum make-up and twisted the length of her hair into a knot atop her head. Stilettos completed the outfit and she collected a shoulder-bag, caught Nicki's hand, then together they descended the stairs to the foyer.

She met Marcello's speculative gaze with equanimity, glimpsed the faint gleam apparent in those dark eyes and lifted her head fractionally.

'Ready?'

An innuendo? For battle, or the afternoon ahead. She decided to be generous and go with the latter.

Ramon appeared to be enjoying a reasonable day, and Nicki regaled him with her exploits at the Aquopolis, and her excitement at visiting Madrid city.

The elderly man's pleasure in his great-granddaughter's company was reciprocal, and despite the tremendous age difference their mutual rapport was something to see.

Even short visits tended to tire Ramon, and they took their leave when his attendant nurse indicated he should rest.

Once they were seated in the Porsche four-wheel-drive Marcello handed Shannay a leather folder.

'For your use.'

Inside the zipped compartment was a list of numbers, personal, business and emergency. A bank account and affiliated high-end credit card in the name of Shannay Martinez.

Definite overkill for a sojourn lasting a matter of weeks.

She looked at him carefully, and was unable to discern anything from his expression. 'Thank you,' she acknowledged quietly. 'But I have money of my own.'

His eyes speared hers, dark and impossibly enigmatic, and for a moment she thought he meant to insist. Instead he merely inclined his head.

'Your prerogative.'

She turned her attention to Nicki as Marcello pointed out places of interest.

Madrid city bore little change. Brilliant architecture vied with the old, and there was an air of timelessness, of great history.

Carlo dropped them off and moved on to find parking, while Marcello settled Nicki into the curve of one arm.

Exclusive boutiques were dotted along the Calle de Serrano and interconnecting avenues, bearing ruinously expensive designer labels so far beyond her budget there seemed little point engaging the vendeuse's attention.

Except what was a visit to Madrid city without viewing the superb leather-goods, the shoes and bags? Or window-shopping at Las Perlas, Loewe's and Prada?

Carlo met up with them, and together he and Marcello flanked her as they strolled and browsed.

It brought to mind the clothes Marcello had insisted on gifting her during the early years of her marriage...all of which she'd left behind. Had he consigned them to charity?

Nicki enjoyed the overall view from her vantage position held in the curve of her father's arm, and there were purchases Marcello insisted on making.

His prerogative, he insisted as he gifted his daughter a beautiful dress, cropped trousers, tops and shoes.

Shannay's protest was ignored, and she didn't have the heart to deny Nicki so much pleasure.

The shops closed their doors at eight, and Marcello selected a café and ordered a light evening meal for Nicki, while he and Carlo drank coffee and Shannay opted for tea.

It was after nine when they reached the La Moraleja mansion, and Marcello carried a visibly wilting Nicki upstairs to her room, where Shannay quickly bathed and tucked her into bed.

The thought of eating a meal comprising more than a light salad didn't appeal, and for a moment she looked longingly at her own bed, barely resisting the temptation to shed her own clothes, shower and slip beneath the bedcovers.

Except Marcello would come find her, and she didn't feel inclined to clash verbal swords with him tonight.

Spanish mealtimes were unusually late by Australian standards, and she picked at the succulent salad, refused a portion of excellent sirloin and selected a delectable peach in lieu of dessert.

'Thank you for gifting Nicki her new clothes.'

'My pleasure.' He doubted she realised just how much it meant to see the wonder in his daughter's eyes, her joy at receiving gifts, and the small arms that wound round his neck in childish gratitude.

It was beyond price, the unconditional love of a child. His child. A child he had no intention of giving up for months at a time while she resided with her mother on the other side of the world.

The meal came to its conclusion, and Marcello excused himself with the need to spend some time in his home office, and Shannay began transferring the table's contents into the kitchen.

Upstairs she checked on Nicki, then she crossed through to her own room and stripped down to her briefs, removed her make-up, then she slid between the sheets.

It was there Marcello found her two hours later, and he stood regarding her recumbent form with a degree of musing exasperation.

And need. Damnable need for the one woman who vowed she didn't want him. Only to have her come alive beneath his touch.

With care he reached down, lifted her into his arms and carried her to his bed, all too aware of her near-naked form, the soft silkiness of her skin and the desire hardening his body.

CHAPTER TEN

THE ENSUING FEW DAYS followed a similar pattern with morning visits with Ramon, followed by an outing for Nicki's benefit with Carlo in attendance.

Together they spent hours at the Warner Bros Park at San Martin de la Vega, and, perhaps the most exciting of all, the Parque de Atracciones.

A magical time for a child, Shannay accorded indulgently as Nicki fell asleep each night before the first page was turned of her bedtime story.

As to the nights… Attempting to sleep in her own suite, only to find herself waking in Marcello's bed, became an exercise in futility. Accepting she was no match for her husband irked unbearably.

Eventually she admitted defeat and slid into his bed at the end of another tiring day.

Where she stayed. Not, she assured herself, because she *wanted* to…merely to prove she could lie within touching distance and *sleep*…eventually.

She just wickedly hoped he *suffered.*

As she did, when he gathered her close…yet made no further move. A hand that slid to her breast…and remained still. Or rested on her hip, and stayed there.

Was he deliberately testing her?

Maybe she should respond in kind and test *him*.

Except such a move could be tricky. What if he divined it as an indicative sanction for sex?

Then she would not only lose the battle, she'd also lose the war.

And that would never do.

The weekend brought Marcello's obligatory attendance at a gala event lauded by the city's scions.

Invitation only, black tie, and Shannay was apprised of the need to wear something *stunning* by Penè, who had stopped by the mansion to visit Nicki.

The unspoken message was very clear, and racked up Shannay's nervous tension to unbelievable heights during a shopping expedition the day before with Marcello's aunt in attendance for *the* gown, stilettos and accessories.

It was an indisputable fact that Penè *knew* fashion as they progressed from one boutique to another, and they eventually settled on a dream of a gown by Armani in pale peach and apricot silk chiffon. Full-length, the skirt was cut on the bias and bore a clever bias-cut overlay in peach over apricot. A silk chiffon stole added an extra elegance, and Shannay could only applaud Penè's selection.

Exquisite evening sandals and matching evening bag were added to the growing collection Carlo stowed in the back of the Porsche.

Penè was in her element, clearly revelling in playing the *grande dame* with the various *vendeuses,* and enjoying their obsequious attention.

Shannay found it all a bit much as the evening closing hours drew near.

'Minimum jewellery,' Marcello's aunt stated. 'The gown requires little enhancement. Your hair should be confined in a sleek style, definitely not loose. Understated make-up with emphasis on the eyes and mouth.'

'I agree.'

'You look peaky.' Penè eyes were piercing above her patrician nose. 'Is my nephew keeping you awake nights?'

Oh, my. A *yes* or *no* would be an equally incriminating response.

The look sharpened. 'Are you pregnant?'

Now that was a definite negative. 'No.'

'You should have another child,' Penè said bluntly. 'Marcello needs a son to take the Martinez name into the next generation.'

She couldn't help herself. 'He already has a daughter.'

'A son,' Penè insisted imperiously. 'Named Ramon, in honour of my father.'

'What if I were to consider filing for divorce?' She chose not to reveal she'd already set the legalities in motion.

'Divorce for a Martinez isn't an option. Marcello would refuse to countenance such a thing.' She looked suitably astonished. 'Foolish girl. What are you thinking? He can give you everything you desire.'

Except the one thing I want.

His heart.

I gave him mine, unconditionally…only to discover he didn't value it.

'I think we're done,' Shannay said aloud. She even managed a faint smile as Carlo added another emblem-emblazoned designer bag to their mounting collection.

Carlo delivered Penè to Ramon's residence, then continued to La Moraleja.

Nicki was tucked in bed with Marcello seated on its edge as he read from a storybook when Shannay entered the bedroom.

Attired in black jeans and a black chambray shirt, he looked totally at ease, and she tamped down the emotional reaction stirring deep within at the mere sight of him.

Pheronomes, intense sexual awareness…it was attraction at its most dangerous, and need, basic and earthy, pulsed through her body.

She remembered only too well when she had only to look at him to witness the secret promise in those dark eyes, and know how the night would end…as it almost always did.

A time when they couldn't get enough of each other.

Until the doubts crept in, and everything began to change.

'Mummy!'

There was time out for a mutual kiss and a hug before Nicki settled back against the pillow.

'Daddy and me went swimming in the pool. And I've had dinner and a bath.' Brown eyes widened. 'And I cleaned my teeth.'

'Well done,' Shannay said with warmth, including both man and child, and incurred a studied appraisal. 'Thanks,' she added quietly.

'No problem.' He glimpsed the faint edge of pain, the aftermath of several hours in Penè's company. 'A productive afternoon?'

'I'm sure we maxed your credit card.'

A faint smile tugged the edges of his mouth. 'Doubtful.'

Yes, she supposed it was, and she added— 'Thank you. Penè's help was invaluable.'

But tiring, he deduced, all too aware of his aunt's incessant need to constantly verbalise with an opinion on everything in an often uncompromising manner.

'Can I see what you bought?'

Marcello leant forward and lightly touched Nicki's cheek. 'In the morning, *pequena*. Now let's find out what happens to Cinderella, shall we?'

'She goes to the ball and comes home in a pumpkin,' Nicki relayed solemnly, and Marcello smiled.

'I think you've heard this story before.'

'It's my favourite.'

One of many, Shannay reflected as she sat down on the opposite side of the bed while Marcello finished reading, by which time Nicki had fallen asleep, and Shannay turned down the light and preceded him from the room.

'I'll go change, then meet you downstairs.' The thought of food held little appeal. Given a choice she'd prefer to eat at the time of the late-afternoon *merienda,* as Nicki did.

A quick shower proved refreshing, and she slipped into dress jeans, pulled on a short-sleeved rib-knit top in a deep coral, twisted her hair into a loose knot, then added lipgloss.

Dinner comprised a light omelette with salad, followed by fresh fruit, during the eating of which they caught up on their individual afternoon activities.

'Penè was suitably restrained?'

Shannay took a careful sip of water and replaced the glass down onto the table before directing Marcello a pensive look.

'You want polite?'

He pushed his plate to one side and viewed her with speculative interest. 'I'm very familiar with my aunt's penchant for plain speaking.'

'In essence, I'm peaky…the cause of which must be you keeping me awake nights, or I'm pregnant. Preferably the latter, as it's my duty to provide you with another child. A son.'

Marcello sank back in his chair. 'I'm intrigued to hear your response.'

'Let's just say it invoked the reminder a Martinez would never countenance divorce.'

His eyes seared her own. 'You can have whatever you want, Shannay…with one exception. A divorce.'

A sudden lump rose in her throat, and she swallowed it carefully. 'I don't want gifts, haute couture or a high-profile social life. They mean nothing to me. They never did.'

'Yet we share the gift of a child.'

'The one thing I won't let you take away from me,' Shannay vowed with renewed fervour, and something flickered in the depths of his eyes before it was successfully masked.

'It was never my intention to do so.'

'Yet you'd consign us both to a convenient marriage where we maintain a façade in public?' Her eyes darkened, and pain curled deep inside. 'For what purpose, Marcello?' She drew in a slightly ragged breath. 'Revenge…because I didn't inform you of Nicki's existence?'

'Is that what you think?'

'I think you're playing a game,' she flung, sorely tried as she rose to her feet.

Dignity and pride. She possessed both, and she walked away from him without a further glance, uncaring whether he followed or not.

Sleep proved elusive, and she tossed and turned, only to slip out of bed and take something to ease a tension headache.

Eventually she must have slept, for she came awake aware she was no longer in her own bed, but held in strong masculine arms as Marcello traversed the dimly lit gallery *en route* to his own suite.

'Put me down!' Her voice was little more than a sibilant hiss as she struggled against him.

Without success, and she balled a fist and lashed out uncaring as to where it landed.

In a matter of seconds he entered the suite, closed the door behind him, then released her down to stand in front of him.

Shannay glared at him in open defiance, hating him in that instant as she ignored the darkness evident in his eyes and the bunched muscle at the edge of his jaw.

'This is ridiculous. You're *impossible!*' She released a growl of frustration.

'That's the best you can do?'

She ignored his indolent drawl, the waiting, watching quality in his stance…and launched into a barely restrained diatribe that used every emotive adjective she could recall.

One eyebrow slanted as she came to a halt, and he posed silkily, 'You're done?'

'*Yes,* dammit!'

'Good.'

He captured her shoulders and drew her in, then he closed his mouth over her own, took all the fiery heat and tamed it, ignoring her flailing fists as they faltered and fell to her sides.

He wanted her unbidden response, and deliberately sought it, sensing the low groan deep in her throat as she fought against capitulation. Followed soon after by the involuntary slide of her tongue against his own, the sudden hitch in her breath as she angled her head and allowed him free access.

One hand slid to her nape, while the other moved down her back, bunched the oversized T-shirt and slipped beneath the cotton fabric to cup and gently squeeze her bottom.

His body tightened unbearably and he lifted her, eased her thighs apart, then positioned her to accept his fully aroused length as he eased into the slick, welcoming heat, heard her faint sigh…and surged in to the hilt.

Then it was his turn to bite back a guttural sound as her vaginal muscles enclosed him, and he began to move, creating a rhythm that sent them both high until they reached the brink, then soared together in a shattering climax.

At some stage Marcello had dispensed with her T-shirt, although she had no recollection of *when,* only that she was naked in his arms and his lips were tantalising hers, nibbling and teasing until she held fast his head and kissed him with such exquisite eroticism he was hard-pressed not to take her again.

Instead he crossed to the bed, eased down onto his back with her sitting astride him.

Her mouth was softly swollen, and his eyes darkened as she lifted both hands and tucked her hair behind each ear. The movement lifted her breasts, and he traced their soft curves, teased the tender peaks…and watched her eyes glaze over.

They were both at each other's mercy, and she shifted deliberately, glimpsed the increasing darkness apparent in his gleaming gaze, then she gave a startled cry as he brought her down and took one tender peak into his mouth.

Intense pleasure spiralled through her body as he suckled, and a warning hiss escaped from her lips as he caught the swollen bud between his teeth and rolled it to the point beyond pleasure to the imminent edge of pain.

It made her acutely vulnerable, and she opened her mouth to plead with him, only for the pressure to ease as he soothed the tender peak.

Then he wrapped his arms around her slender frame and rolled until she lay beneath him. For a moment he drank in the sight of her, the wildness of her hair, the sensual glow warming her skin, and the magical passion they shared.

She moistened her lips, and he drove into her only to almost withdraw before repeating the action again and again, increasing the intensity of the rhythm until she joined him in a climax more shattering than the first.

Afterwards he gathered her close and rested his lips against her temple in the lazy afterglow of spent passion.

Shannay was close to sleep when he manoeuvred her onto her tummy and began a wonderfully soothing massage of her neck and shoulders, easing out the kinks there before slipping down to knead her calf muscles and finally her feet.

His lips pressed a trail of light kisses over her leg, bit gently into the globe of her bottom, then eased up to her nape.

She turned into him and rested her mouth into the curve at the base of his throat, murmured something indistinct, then drifted into deep sleep.

The gala event held in one of the city's splendid theatres appeared to be a sell-out, with numerous fashionistas vying for supremacy in designer gowns and exquisite jewellery.

The *crème de la crème* of Madrid society, patrons of the arts, who paid an exorbitant ticket price to attend the evening's classical production.

In pairs, small groups, they gathered in the large foyer, and Shannay stood at Marcello's side with a ready smile in place as guests mixed and mingled.

Tall, dark, impeccably groomed, his evening suit a perfect tailored fit, pristine white shirt and black bow-tie, he looked the epitome of the powerful, sophisticated male.

He stood out from the rest. Not so much for his attractive features or his clothing, but for the primitive aura he projected beneath the hard-muscled frame…a disruptive sensuality that threatened much and promised to deliver.

It drew women to him like bees to a honeypot, and there were those who simply adored to flirt, while a few made moves, subtle and not so subtle, to attract his attention.

In the early days of their marriage she'd hugged to her heart the knowledge he was *hers,* believing nothing and no one could harm what they shared.

How naive she had been!

'Ah, there you are.'

Shannay turned and met Penè's encompassing appraisal, caught the brief nod of approval and leant forward to bestow the obligatory air-kiss to each cheek.

'How is Ramon?'

'Fading. The physician expects him to lapse into a coma within the next few days. Sandro and Luisa are with him.'

Such an incredibly sad end for a man who had once headed the Martinez empire.

'I'm so sorry.' Shannay's empathy was genuine, and Marcello's aunt inclined her head in acknowledgment.

'Tonight may well be the last public engagement at which the family appear. The usual mourning period will understandably be observed.'

'Of course.'

'I must greet Pablo and Angelique Santanas,' Penè announced, and melted into the crowd.

Soon the massive doors swung open and the guests gradually drifted into the auditorium to take their seats.

The classical performance proved superb, with brilliant costumes and high-tempo music. Stirring, passionate, with a touch of pathos.

A break between Act I and II proved welcome, so too when the curtain came down after the second act.

'Can I get you something to drink?' Marcello asked as they entered the foyer.

'Anything chilled and non-alcoholic,' Shannay requested with a faint smile, and watched as he signalled a hovering waiter.

It was only a matter of minutes later when she turned slightly and saw Estella moving towards them.

Oh, *joy.*

The woman resembled a picture-perfect Latin doll attired in a Spanish-inspired chiffon gown in stunning red and white diagonal chiffon frills that moved with exquisite fluidity at every step she took.

Sexy, Shannay accorded silently. Very deliberately sexy, from the top of her gloriously coiffured head to the tip of her beautiful lacquered toenails in matching red.

'Shannay.' The greeting was polite, brief, then Estella gave Marcello her full attention.

'*Querido.*'

Could a woman's voice purr?

Definitely.

'Estella.'

Hmm, was that a tinge of warning beneath Marcello's pleasant tone?

Play polite, Shannay bade silently as she summoned a smile and offered an innocuous remark...which Estella totally ignored.

'We are thinking of going on to a nightclub afterwards. Perhaps you'd care to join us?'

'Thank you. No,' Marcello responded civilly, and the woman offered a convincing pout.

'Your wife—' she gave the word a faint emphasis and touched a lacquered nail to the lapel of his jacket '—accompanies you, and you become less fun.'

'Perhaps,' Marcello drawled, carefully removing her hand, 'my wife provides all the fun I need.'

Estella cast Shannay a look that contained thinly veiled mockery. 'Indeed?'

In some instances silence was golden, Shannay perceived. This wasn't one of them.

'Marcello is a superb tutor. Don't you agree?'

Estella's gaze shifted to Marcello as she ran the tip of her tongue over her upper lip and offered a knowing smile. 'The best, darling.'

It's an act, she qualified. A deliberate attempt to undermine.

Four years ago she would have taken the bait.

Now she simply offered quietly, 'Yet he chose not to marry you. Why was that, do you suppose?'

The faint disbelief evident before it was quickly masked should have brought a sense of satisfaction.

Except instinct warned Shannay that Estella would merely choose her moment for the next verbal strike.

'Possibly I decided he wasn't the best *marriage* material?' She waited a few seconds, then honed in sweetly, 'Isn't that why you left him?'

Bitch.

If she asserted Marcello hunted her down, she'd leave herself open for Estella to drag Nicki into the verbal equation, and she refused to allow that.

'No.'

The supercilious arched eyebrow did it.

Forget politeness. 'Go find your husband, Estella.' The silent implication "and leave mine alone" was clearly evident.

The mocking smile conceded nothing as the socialite turned with a slow, deliberately sensual movement and began weaving her way through the gathered patrons.

'Your support was gratifying,' Shannay noted quietly, unsure whether she was pleased or relieved, and bore his appraisal.

'You were doing so well on your own.'

'She's a—'

'*Femme fatale,*' Marcello drawled. 'Who thrives on playing games with the vulnerable.'

Her chin tilted and her eyes lanced his own. 'The term *vulnerable* no longer applies to me.'

Marcello cast her a musing glance as he caught hold of her hand and brushed a soothing thumb over the veins at her wrist, where the quickened beat of her pulse belied her contrived air of calm.

The intervening years had provided a level of maturity and independence he could only admire.

With every passing day his desire for revenge lessened, and it irked him, for he wanted to make her pay for denying him the experience of her pregnancy, the birth, and his daughter's infancy.

There was still a degree of anger beneath the surface vying with an overpowering physical need he fought hard to control.

As she did.

Two opposing forces caught up with events of the past, and fighting to reconcile their future.

A future he was determined to secure.

Shannay felt a sense of relief when it came time to be seated for the third and final act.

Marcello enclosed her hand in his throughout, and his fingers merely tightened whenever she tried to withdraw.

Once he lifted their joined hands to his lips, brushed hers lightly, then rested them on his lap, and her heart jumped and refused to settle for what seemed an age.

His arousal beneath the conventional clothing was a potent hidden force, and it took considerable effort to focus on the players on the stage as the act progressed towards its conclusion.

She didn't move, could barely bear to breathe, and she was never more glad of the theatre's darkened interior.

Dear heaven, did his aunt notice?

She sincerely hoped not, and refused to glance in Penè's direction.

It was a tremendous relief when the curtain came down, then rose again to applause, and the lights came on.

Exiting the auditorium became a slow process, noisy with audience chatter against muted background recorded music, and there was the obligatory pause or ten when they reached the foyer and moved towards the main entrance.

Penè bade them goodnight as her car and driver pulled into the kerb, followed minutes later as Carlo eased their own car to a halt.

They were scarcely seated when Marcello reached for her hand and threaded his fingers through her own.

Shannay attempted to free them without success, and she looked at him in silent askance.

What was he doing?

They had no audience, no one to impress with their pretended togetherness.

Twice she endeavoured to pull free during the drive to La Moraleja, and he refused to allow her to succeed.

When they reached the mansion he drew her indoors, then he simply lifted her over one shoulder and made for the stairs.

'What in hell are you playing at?'

'Taking you to bed.'

'I can walk,' she assured his back in scandalous tones, and heard his husky laughter.

'Humour me.'

'Aren't you in the least wary I might kick you where it hurts?'

'Don't try it, *querida*. You'll spoil the fun, and I can promise you won't like my retaliation.'

'Fun? You think it's *fun* being hauled around like a sack of potatoes?'

They reached the gallery and, at its end, the master suite, where he slid her down to her feet.

Without a word he caught her close and kissed her...gently at first, savouring the taste and texture of her lips, her mouth. Then with a sensual intensity that reached right down and took hold of her soul.

She was helpless, mindless, and barely aware of his fingers releasing the zip fastening on her dress...until it slithered to the floor in a silken heap. Her bra came next, followed by the satin briefs, and she gasped as he cupped her breast and lowered his mouth to suckle its peak.

A hand slid down over her stomach and sought the moist warmth at the apex of her thighs, and the breath hitched in her throat.

'Undress me.'

He helped her dispense with his clothes, his shoes, as she slid out of stilettos, then he lifted her onto the bed and moved down beside her.

The trail of his lips followed the same path as his fingers as he brought her to climax again and again, until she cried out, begging for the release only he could give.

It was then he sought the moist heat with his fully engorged penis and thrust in to the hilt in one forceful movement, waited until she caught her breath, and sought the familiar rhythm that sent them both soaring to unbelievable heights, held them there in a spectacular climax, then tipped them over the brink in a slow, sensual free-fall.

Later, much later, she gifted him a tasting that left the breath hissing through his clenched teeth, and tested his control to the limit.

It was her turn to cry out as he pulled her on top of him and took her for the ride of her life.

CHAPTER ELEVEN

Two days later Ramon slipped into a coma, from which he never recovered, and his funeral was a private family occasion, followed by a memorial service attended by close friends, family and captains of industry.

It was an infinitely sad time for them all, especially Penè who went into a decline and cancelled everything on her social calendar for an unspecified time.

Ramon's will distributed his considerable personal fortune equally between Penè, Marcello, Sandro...and Nicki.

Marcello and Shannay were named as Nicki's trustees, and the inheritance made their daughter a very rich little girl.

Marcello's presence was required in the city on frequent occasions during the ensuing week. Days when he left early and returned late, sometimes long after Nicki had fallen asleep.

To compensate he rang and spoke to his daughter through the day and again before she went to bed.

Shannay filled the days as best she could, supervising Nicki with her swimming, reading, finger-painting and constructing models with play-dough.

She also offered to assist Penè in any way possible, without success.

'Leave her grieve,' Marcello advised when she broached

it one evening after he arrived home late. 'She needs to come to terms with Ramon's death in her own time, in her own way.'

She looked at him carefully, noting the lines fanning out from the corners of his eyes seemed more pronounced, the grooves slashing his cheeks a little deeper.

'And you, Marcello?'

'Concerned for me, *querida?*'

'Perhaps. A little.'

He discarded his suit jacket, loosened his tie, toed off his shoes, then he reached for her, pulling her close to kiss her deeply, taking his time before he lifted his mouth from her own.

'Come share my shower.'

She tilted her head to one side and regarded him thoughtfully. 'That could be dangerous.'

His eyes gleamed and he gave a husky chuckle. 'So take the risk and live a little.'

'In the shower?'

His fingers slid to the hem of her singlet top and pulled it free from the waistband of her jeans, stripped her of it in one easy movement, then he undid the clip on her bra.

'Since when has that presented a problem?'

He reached for the snap on her jeans, slid the zip down and eased the denim over her hips.

It felt so good to have his hands shape her slender form, to drift his fingers over the highly sensitive curve at the base of her neck, the touch of his lips to her nape, the gentle tactile exploration that unfurled a capricious sexuality and became raw with hunger…for him, only him.

He branded her with his mouth, the edges of his teeth in a coupling that was explosive, primitive as he demanded her compliance and made her his own.

It said much as she lost herself in him and became greedy,

meeting him with each thrust as she urged him almost to a point of savagery, and she held on, soaring with him to unbelievable heights in a sexual climax more pagan than any they'd previously shared.

Afterwards he simply rested his cheek against her temple as their breathing slowed, and the water cascaded over their bodies slick with sexual sweat.

He said something in Spanish beneath his breath, then trailed his mouth down to capture hers in a kiss so incredibly gentle, her eyes shimmered with emotive tears.

With care, he took the soap and smoothed it over her body, his eyes dark and impossibly slumberous as he caught the faint pink smudges marking her tender flesh.

When he was done, she took the soap from his hand and returned the favour, exulting in the hard musculature, olive skin darker than her own, and the inherent masculinity that was intensely male and his alone.

It took a while before they pulled on towelling robes and emerged into the bedroom.

Her cellphone beeped intermittently, alerting a text message, and a slight frown creased her forehead as she read the text.

'Anything urgent?' Marcello queried as he discarded the robe and slid naked between the bedcovers.

'It's John,' she relayed slowly, meeting his gaze. 'He wants to know when he can expect me back.'

His eyes darkened, and he went completely still. 'You won't be returning to Perth.'

Shannay opened her mouth, then closed it again. 'Marcello, my job, my life, everything is there.'

'It was never *there* from the moment I discovered Nicki's existence.'

Oh, dear lord. 'You don't understand,' she protested, feeling sick and slightly stricken as she took in his hardened features.

'Make me understand,' Marcello began in a dangerously silky tone. 'How you can lose yourself in my arms night after night…and yet still want to leave.'

He had her there, and she felt suddenly bereft of words. Too ashamed to admit he held the power to render her wanton and solely his. To need him as a flower in the desert craved water in order to survive.

That without him, she simply existed.

'You asked me to stay longer for Ramon's sake, and I have.'

Say it, she begged silently. Say you care. Tell me I mean something to you.

'Leaving isn't an option.' The reiteration held an adamant non-negotiation hardness that chilled her to the bone.

There was only one thing she could do, and she tightened the belt on her robe and moved to the door.

'I'll sleep in another room.'

It killed her to walk through the door and close it quietly behind her.

Stupid tears gathered and rolled slowly down each cheek as she traversed the gallery to the suite she'd occupied during the initial few days after her arrival.

For some reason she needed to check on Nicki, to see her sweet face in sleep, and try to quantify her wayward emotions.

The dim night-light revealed a child at peace, silently trusting, and so much a part of her just the thought brought an ache to her throat.

Nicki was happy here…and hadn't that been the object of this excursion?

A visit, to help Nicki adjust to spending time with her father. Thinly disguised custody posing as holidays.

Preparation for what the future would involve.

Shannay had never in her wildest imagination expected the visit to be anything else.

Yet she hadn't counted on being so acutely vulnerable to the father of her child. Or to remember so vividly what they'd shared.

She'd been a fool. Incredibly naive not to foresee maintaining a formal relationship couldn't last long.

Had he knowingly plotted just this outcome? Planned to seduce her and force her to stay?

Even get her pregnant?

It was a long time before she fell into an uneasy sleep, and late next morning when she woke.

Nicki was happily ensconsed in the kitchen beneath Maria's care, and relayed Marcello had left early for the city.

There was a need to do something constructive with the day, preferably away from the house.

Shopping held no appeal but, recalling how much Nicki had loved the children's section of the Parque de Attracciones, Shannay thought it would be great to enjoy a return visit.

With Carlo in attendance, of course.

It was relatively easy to arrange, and they set off with a delighted little girl whose excitement became infectious as the day progressed.

The rides, the people, the other children and the carnival-like atmosphere helped diminish Shannay rehashing the fall-out from John's text message.

How could she remain in Madrid when there were unresolved issues?

Worse, how could she bear to stay in a marriage simply because of *convenience?* Even more disturbing…consider adding another child?

It wasn't enough to *pretend*. To attempt to believe the marriage was alive and healthy simply because the sex was good.

Oh, tell it like it is, why don't you? It's fantastic…off the Richter scale.

She'd been there, suffered, and thrown in the towel.

Why put herself through it again?

Except you're already in over your head.

Admit it.

Something…instinct, maternal or otherwise, alerted her attention.

Nicki. Where was *Nicki?*

Fear, panic, both meshed into something incredibly frightening as she consciously searched for the red top and cropped jeans Nicki was wearing, the bright red bow in her hair…felt her heart leap when she thought she caught a glimpse of red, only to have her hopes dashed seconds later.

Carlo? Where in hell was Carlo?

How could they *both* be missing?

'Please, have you seen a little girl…' She began frantically questioning one stranger after another, some of the children…in a mixture of English and Spanish as she described Nicki and her clothing…to which she received visual concern, the shake of a head, *nothing.*

Oh, dear God. She prayed, made deals with the deity, and in a moment of common sense extracted her cellphone and rang Marcello's private number on speed dial.

He picked up on the second tone, listened to her garbled explanation and issued an icily calm directive.

'Stay where you are. I'm on my way.'

He immediately excused himself from an important meeting, made a personal call to the chief of police, issued orders to various staff as he had his car brought kerb-side in front of the building's main entrance, and he attempted to make contact with Carlo.

By the time he arrived at the *parque,* he'd gathered an overview of the situation…and Carlo's cellphone had been switched off.

So too had the personal tracking device he carried at all times when leaving the house.

Two factors which sent alarm bells screaming inside Marcello's head.

Nicki's existence had been kept as low-profile as possible. Except it didn't take a mathematician to work out the value of a child with direct connections to the Martinez dynasty. Factor in Ramon's recent demise, and the value accelerated a thousandfold.

The abductors had to be professionals. Carlo was the best, and if they'd slipped beneath his alert surveillance it had to be a highly planned operation.

Shannay saw Marcello the instant he came into view, and she looked at him in silent desperation as he joined her.

There was little evident in his expression as he gathered her close, and one glance at her pale features was sufficient for him to reassure,

'Don't blame yourself.'

Then he began firing questions over the top of her head.

His presence did little to ease the panic pumping through her body. She was too stunned to cry, too inwardly frozen to do more than operate on some form of automatic pilot as police joined the *parque's* security personnel.

The majority of their rapid Spanish went beyond her comprehension, and she stood at Marcello's side, endeavouring to dismiss numerous images too horrifying to contemplate.

How could Marcello deal with the situation with such apparent *calm?*

Shannay searched his features, caught the clenched muscle at the edge of his jaw, heard the tightness in his voice…and exchanged calm for control.

There would be a phone call.

Wasn't that how a kidnapping unfolded?

She was a total mess, mentally and emotionally, desperately wanting to rewind the clock, wishing she hadn't taken her eye off Nicki for a second.

For that was all it had taken.

'Carlo? Who are these men?' Nicki's small hand tightened within his own. 'Where are they taking us?'

Carlo was wired, he'd already activated the panic button, but any minute soon they'd pat him down…and any existing contact would be lost.

The important thing was to protect his charge. To minimise the impact of the kidnapping and to remain alert for any eventuality.

'Just a little ride, *pequena,*' he assured gently. 'It's OK.'

His training served him well, and no one, especially the child whose trust in him at this moment was unconditional, guessed beneath his calm persona there was a concealed Glock aimed right at his kidney.

They reached a nondescript dark-coloured van, the rear doors opened and Carlo lifted Nicki and deposited her on the metal floor.

'There aren't any seats to sit on,' Nicki whispered as he leaned in close.

He watched her eyes widen as he spread his arms and legs wide…hiding, he hoped, the fact he was being competently searched, his sports watch taken in case it contained an alert device.

A guttural oath sounded from behind as the taped wire was discovered, and he clenched his teeth as it was wrenched free. Then a hard metal object slammed into his kidneys, his hands were cuffed and he was pushed into the van, managing by reflex action to roll into an upright position without making a sound. Difficult when suffering excruciating pain.

'I don't like those men.'

Neither did he.

The doors slammed shut, he heard the lock catch, followed seconds later by the faint throb of the engine.

'We're going on an adventure,' Carlo offered gently. 'Shall I tell you a story?'

There was a tiny electronic device in his shoe. Virtually a panic button, which when activated provided a direct link to the police. As long as the device remained undetected, it would allow the police to track their whereabouts.

It wouldn't be too difficult to extract, but he couldn't risk Nicki asking what he was doing.

On the off-chance a listening device was planted inside the van, he lifted his cuffed hands to his face and pressed a finger to his lips.

Nicki copied his action and nodded.

Good. She'd remembered the few basic alerts he'd offered in explanation of why he always accompanied members of her family, instilling gently he would always win and she should never be frightened.

He began to intone a nursery rhyme as he quietly worked, controlling the slow slide as the van took a corner, the pause as it halted at a traffic intersection.

Their abductors were taking no chances, he perceived, for their speed was regulated, normal, and they were heading in a northerly direction.

There was a sense of satisfaction when he freed the electronic device, then once it was activated he replaced it carefully out of sight.

By now, Shannay would have alerted Marcello, notified the police…and it was only a matter of time.

He gave Nicki an indicative victory sign, and moved from one story to another. Heaven help him, he even sang a few songs, silently encouraging Nicki to join in…which, bless her brave little heart, she did.

It would take time to set up a roadblock, and his main objective was providing sufficient distraction to prevent Nicki from becoming too frightened.

Together they discussed her favourite stories, and *Shrek* the movie, Fiona, Puss in Boots and Donkey.

Once, she lifted hands and wiped tears from her cheek. 'When will I see my mummy?'

'Soon, *pequena*. Soon,' he promised, and prayed he was right. 'Your daddy will make sure of it.'

Every minute seemed like an hour, each one the worst and the longest in Shannay's life.

Nothing else came close.

Then two things happened almost simultaneously.

Marcello's cellphone rang…and seconds later he smiled.

Hope soared as she waited anxiously for him to relay news, and when he did it was all she could do not to subside in a heap.

Nicki was safe.

Carlo had her.

Their abductors had been forced to a halt at a police road-block on the northern outskirts.

Nicki was in Carlo's care, and their abductors were under arrest.

Reaction, immense relief…the emotional fall-out from a living nightmare began to have an effect, and tears welled up and spilled to run silently down each cheek.

Marcello took one look and cradled her face between his hands, easing the warm moisture with each thumb.

'Nicki is fine. They're on their way home in a police car. We'll meet them there.'

She wasn't capable of uttering so much as a word, and he lowered his head to hers and pressed his lips to each eyelid in turn.

A gesture which only increased the flow of tears, and his mouth closed over her own in a brief, evocative kiss before he lifted his head.

'Let's go home, hmm?'

Shannay was grateful for the arm he curved across the back of her waist as he led her to his car. Seated, he spared her a brief glance, glimpsed her still pale features and dark eyes fixed unseeing beyond the windscreen and he swore softly beneath his breath.

'Let it go, *querida*,' he advised gently, and she turned towards him with tear-drenched eyes.

'How can I?' Her mouth quivered with emotion. 'What if Carlo—?' She couldn't say the words. Didn't want to voice them.

'From tomorrow, Carlo will have a partner, and they'll both shadow your every move.'

If he meant to reassure, he failed miserably.

Two bodyguards.

The thought of always needing protection freaked her out. Never being able to make a spontaneous decision.

She didn't want Nicki to grow up always on the defensive, intensely cautious and wary.

Heaven knew what effect this afternoon's episode would have, or the long-term toll it might take.

'I'll ensure it will never happen again,' Marcello vowed quietly, and she shot him a disbelieving look.

'You can't promise that. We both know Nicki has become a target.'

There were choices.

And she knew which one she had to make.

Nicki appeared subdued and clung to each of them in turn the instant they entered the foyer.

Carlo was there, so too was Maria, as well as a plain-clothes policewoman who spent considerable time talking with Nicki. A psychology tool which undoubtedly helped, and afterwards Marcello took Carlo aside for an in-depth rundown of the abduction.

Shannay couldn't bear to let Nicki out of her sight, and she bathed her, then she picked at a salad while encouraging Nicki to eat.

Together with Marcello, they shared reading a bedtime story, and afterwards she remained at Nicki's bedside long after her daughter fell asleep.

It was late when Marcello returned to the room and hunkered down beside the chair.

'Come to bed,' he bade quietly. 'Nicki is perfectly safe.'

'I need to be here if she wakes.'

'The sensors monitor every sound. We'll hear the instant she stirs.'

She looked at him in the dimmed lighting and slowly shook her head. 'I can't.'

He remained silent for several telling seconds, then he rose to his full height and walked from the room.

She wanted to cry, but she was all teared out, and she sat staring into space, living and reliving the afternoon from the moment before Nicki disappeared, trying to pin down something…anything that would provide a visual clue so she could correlate it in her mind with the facts Carlo had relayed.

Shannay wasn't aware of falling asleep, only that she woke with a start, experienced a moment of disorientation before she recognised her whereabouts.

She checked Nicki, then turned towards the chair…only to hesitate. Her neck felt stiff, and she was cold. Not from the room's temperature, but chilled and shaky from emotional exhaustion.

Even in bed she couldn't get warm, and after what seemed an age spent tossing and turning she moved quietly out onto the gallery, contemplated going down to the kitchen to make a cup of tea, then changed her mind.

'Unable to sleep?'

She hadn't heard a sound or sensed any movement, yet Marcello was there, large and indomitable in the dim gallery light.

'I looked in on Nicki, and decided to check on you,' he offered quietly, and uttered a soft imprecation as a shiver shook her slim frame.

With an unconscious movement she wrapped her arms round her midriff in the hope it would minimise the shaking…without success, and the next instant he swept her into his arms and carried her to the master suite.

'I'm fine,' Shannay muttered as he slid into bed and drew her with him.

'Sure you are.' The soft oath whispered in the night air as he began smoothing his hands over her limbs, stimulating circulation with brisk sweeping movements, until the shivering slowly eased and warmth invaded her body.

She should leave, and she meant to…except she was reluctant to part from the compassion he offered, the security of being held in strong arms, and the touch of his lips against her forehead.

It felt so *good* to breathe in the familiar scent of him, the faint tinge of soap he'd used mingling with the muskiness of male.

It crept into her senses, as powerful as any aphrodisiac, stirring alive the hunger for his touch, and she murmured indistinctly as she pressed her lips into the warm skin, savoured a little, then slid her hand down his arm to rest on his hip.

Marcello tilted her chin and sought her mouth with his own, gently at first, taking it slow with an evocative slide of his tongue along her longer lip, felt her mouth part, allowing him entry, and the tentative welcome as her tongue moved to tease his own, sweetly cajoling in an elemental dance that could have only one ending.

He fought to control his arousal, knowing that if he didn't it would be over before it began, and she needed a slow loving, a subtle, drifting touch that took a leisurely path towards fulfilment.

This was all about comfort and reassurance, before need.

He could give her that.

And he did. With the slow drift of his hand, the soft caress of his lips as he traversed every sensitive pulse-point, each hollow, pausing to suckle at the tightened bud at the peak of her breast, the tender swell beneath, and low over her quivering stomach to the curls at the apex of her thighs.

Lower, as he explored the sweet moistness, the delicious scent of woman and the swollen clitoris pulsing beneath the erotic laving of his tongue.

Her fingers threaded through his hair, then curled into its length and tugged as sensation spiralled through her body. She arched, unconsciously craving more…and he obliged, cradling her hips between his hands as he held her still.

She was his, mind, body and soul, and still he held back, exerting taut control as she shattered beneath his touch.

Marcello eased her into his arms, cradling her shuddering form as she buried her face into the curve of his neck…and when she went to move, he tightened his hold.

'Stay,' he bade huskily. 'I need you like this.'

It was so easy to let her eyelids drift closed, to relax and let the darkness of sleep steal over her.

For a long time he simply held her, lulled by the evenness of her breathing, the soft sigh of her breath warm against his skin…and on the edge of sleep he wondered what the new day would bring.

CHAPTER TWELVE

DESPITE EVERY EFFORT to minimise the abduction attempt on Nicki, it still made the news, appearing on television stations and in the newspapers.

Marcello refused all interviews, requesting the media and public respect their privacy. He employed guards to ensure no media representative intruded into the grounds of his mansion, and Shannay kept Nicki indoors away from the zoom lenses of persistent cameramen well-known to use devious means in order to gain the slightest advantage.

Staff were reminded of their signed confidentiality agreement, and Marcello placed Sandro in a position of power in the city office while he worked from home.

Nicki's well-being was a prime focus, and Shannay rarely let her out of her sight. Thanks to Carlo's handling of the abduction attempt itself, his protective reassurance during their captivity in the van and counselling, Nicki appeared to be dealing quite well with the trauma.

Yet it became apparent the media refused to give up, and although they didn't get past the guards it was impossible to ignore reflected sunlight bouncing off the poised camera lenses, and a helicopter bearing a TV-station logo passed overhead at least three times a day in the hope of a photo scoop.

For Shannay, it was the last straw, and on the third day she drew Marcello aside soon after Nicki had settled to sleep.

'We need to talk.'

His eyes narrowed. 'Let's take it in the bedroom, shall we?'

Not the bedroom. It held too many memories, and she needed to be strong. 'I'd prefer the office.'

He regarded her carefully, examining her features and noting the darkness apparent in her beautiful eyes, the exigent determination, and prepared to do civilised battle.

With a smooth movement he indicated the direction of the office. 'By all means.'

On reaching his sanctum, he closed the door behind them and indicated a comfortable leather chair. 'Take a seat.'

And have him tower over her? 'I'd prefer to stand.'

Marcello crossed the room, leant one hip against the executive desk and held her faintly defiant gaze.

'There is something you want to discuss?'

His voice was mild, but there was a studied stillness about him that reminded her of an indolent predator.

Don't falter. Don't allow him to see the slightest chink in your resolve. 'I'm taking Nicki home to Perth.' There, she'd stated her intention. 'I can book a commercial flight, or ask you to organise your private jet.'

He didn't protest, merely stated fact. 'Your home is here.'

Shannay gave a slight shake of her head. 'We have an arrangement, and you gave me your word,' she reminded, holding his steady gaze. 'I insist you honour it.'

'Circumstances have changed.'

Her chin tilted. 'Because you persuaded me to have sex with you?'

Marcello was silent for a few measurable seconds, then one

eyebrow arched in deliberate query. 'Just…sex. Is that what you call what we share?'

'We scratched a mutual itch.' Liar. It was more than that. Much more.

She stood immobile beneath his deliberate appraisal, and she held his gaze as if her life depended on it.

'There's nothing I can say or do that will change your mind?'

Assure your love for me never died. That *love* is the reason you dragged Nicki and me back to Madrid…not a need to avenge the past.

But he remained silent. And she didn't have the courage to lay bare her emotions.

'No.' It was the only word she could manage without risking an inability to control the tremble in her voice.

'You intend to return to Madrid…when?'

This was the hardest thing she'd ever had to do. 'I'll accompany Nicki when she travels to visit with you.' And die a little every time, she added silently.

'That's your final word?'

She couldn't afford to back down, even though the decision was killing her.

Did he know? Or even guess?

Maybe he didn't even care. Sex was…well, sex. And for a man, without love to make it special, almost any woman would do. And any number of women would line up hoping to tempt him into their bed the instant news filtered out his wife had left him…again.

'Yes.' A determined if stoic confirmation.

She searched his features for the slightest sign her decision affected him…and failed to detect a thing.

When she thought of their lovemaking…and it *was* lovemaking, she wanted to burst into ignominious tears that he could brush it aside so easily.

'When do you plan to leave?'

He wasn't going to argue? Attempt to persuade her to stay? Yet what had she expected? For him to break down and beg? That wasn't his style.

'As soon as possible.'

He didn't move. He merely inclined his head. 'I'll instruct my pilot to have the jet ready tomorrow.'

'Thank you.'

She had to get out of here, away from him, before she broke down, and she turned towards the door.

'What do you plan on telling our daughter?'

It took tremendous effort to look back at him. 'The truth.'

With that she opened the door, passed through the aperture, then quietly closed the door behind her.

A week later Shannay conceded life had begun to slip into its former pattern.

The apartment was aired, cleaned, vacuumed and polished. The pantry, refrigerator and freezer stocked.

Anna appeared delighted to resume evening duties as Nicki's carer, and John was pleased to have her start back at the pharmacy.

She should be happy, content, *relieved* to have left a highly fraught situation behind.

It was, she silently assured, resolved. As originally intended. Hadn't she worked hard to hammer out a satisfactory custody arrangement suitable to Nicki's needs?

Her daughter appeared relatively relaxed, and was looking forward to resuming kindergarten, meeting up with her friends.

Each evening, at the same time, Marcello rang to speak to his daughter and bid her 'goodnight'.

Calls which Nicki eagerly anticipated and received with excited fervour.

The fact he rarely offered more than a restrained greeting to Shannay was immaterial…yet it hurt terribly.

Although what did she expect? Pleasant conversation?

How could he just…switch off, like that?

She shouldn't feel crushed, but she did. It affected her sleep and left her hollow-eyed and aching.

If she didn't soon pull herself together, she'd become a complete and utter emotional mess.

The second week in, she found it difficult to readjust to working the five-to-midnight shift, and John's voiced concern began to rankle.

'I'm fine,' she assured him, and refused to elaborate on the Madrid sojourn.

At the end of the second week confirmation her decree nisi had been granted arrived in the mail from her lawyer.

The decree absolute would follow in approximately one month.

It should have been good news, except it sent her into the depths of despair.

The third week she developed a stomach bug…a persistent one which showed no inclination to subside.

Combined with unaccustomed tiredness and mood swings, the obvious possible reason sent alarm bells skyrocketing through the stratosphere. Consternation provided the need for a pregnancy test, the result of which confirmed her worst fears.

Not so inconceivable when she hadn't used any form of contraceptive following Nicki's birth…nor had Marcello favoured protection.

Fool. What had she been *thinking?*

Worse, what had *he?*

Although, on reflection, *thinking* hadn't even entered the equation!

A fraught twenty-four hours later she redid the pregnancy test, only to have it show the same result.

Ohmigod, *no.* The silent scream seemed to echo inside her brain as she processed the implications in a stark replay.

OK, *think,* she bade shakily, and groaned out loud when she did the calculations and *possible* became *probable,* of which each passing day provided its own confirmation.

Then came the phone call on a week night when she'd cried off work, where Nicki unwittingly informed Marcello "Mummy is sick", and the words were out in spite of Shannay frantically shaking her head.

Seconds later Nicki held out the receiver. 'Daddy wants to talk to you.'

Well, I don't want to talk to him. 'Not now, darling, I'm busy.'

Nicki's eyes rounded in surprise, for Shannay was only folding clothes, and Marcello must have heard, for his voice came clearly through the mouthpiece.

'Take the phone, Shannay.'

She swore softly, and saw her daughter's eyes dilate even further, then she collected the receiver and prepared to play polite.

'Marcello.'

'Nicki said you're unwell.'

Whatever happened to *hello?* She kept her voice even. 'I'm fine.'

'Have you seen a doctor?'

'I'm a pharmacist, remember? I do have a reasonable knowledge of ailments and appropriate medications.'

'Are you pregnant?'

The query came out of left field, and surprised her…although, on reflection, she had to wonder *why*.

'I'm fine,' Shannay reiterated, refusing to fabricate or confirm, then she handed the receiver back to Nicki and exited the room on the pretext of delivering a small stack of folded clothes to the bedroom.

She could hear Nicki's voice in the background, and she moved into the bathroom and began running Nicki's bath.

Employing delaying tactics, she rearranged items on the marble-topped vanity until Nicki entered the bathroom.

'Why didn't you want to talk to Daddy?'

'We talk via email,' she explained carefully as she helped undress her daughter. Brief sentences conveying updates on Nicki.

It took a few days to gather the courage to arrange an appointment with an obstetrician, and she didn't know whether to smile or cry following his examination.

'Congratulations, my dear. You're about halfway through your first trimester.'

The remainder of the day passed in a daze, and she settled Nicki with Anna, then drove to the pharmacy, praying that if they weren't busy she might be able to persuade John to let her finish early.

Shortly after nine she was on the point of considering a tea-break when the electronic buzzer sounded as someone entered the pharmacy.

Shannay glanced up towards the entrance with a ready smile in place…and froze. For walking towards her was the last person she expected to see.

The tall, broad-shouldered male frame was achingly familiar. Attired in black jeans, a white collarless shirt undone at the neck and a butter-soft black leather collarless jacket, Marcello bore a distinct resemblance to a dark warrior.

Why was he here...and why *now?*

All her fine body hairs lifted in sensory recognition, and there was nothing she could do to prevent the surge of blood pulsing through her veins.

It was a magnetic reaction and, try as she might, she was unable to prevent the way she was drawn to him.

His eyes captured and held her own, his features sculptured into almost savage lines, his sensual mouth bracketed by slashing grooves.

He looked dangerous, his eyes almost obsidian in their darkness as he drew close.

Shannay's emotional heart went into meltdown, rendering her almost boneless as she experienced a mix of fear and elation, hope and dismay.

He didn't glance towards John when he spoke, yet the words were for him alone.

'My wife is ceasing work, as of now.'

It wasn't a question, merely a statement of his intent.

Shannay looked at him in shocked surprise. 'You can't just walk in here and—'

'You're leaving.'

'The hell I am.'

'You can walk, or be carried. It's immaterial.'

John started forward. 'Now look here—'

Marcello speared him with a forbidding glance. 'I understand you regard Shannay as a friend. But this is between me and my wife.' He shifted his attention back to Shannay. 'I suggest you collect your keys.'

'No.' The next instant she gave a startled yelp as he reached forward and lifted her over one shoulder, then he indicated the room at the rear of the pharmacy. 'Shannay's be-longings are there?'

What was it between men? Silent signals, male recognition? Whatever, she became aware John retrieved her bag and passed it into Marcello's possession.

'Thank you.' He turned towards the door. 'We'll be in touch.' Then he walked calmly outside, paused beside a limousine, murmured something to the driver, then bundled her into the rear seat.

'What in hell do you think you're doing?' Her voice held restrained fury as he leant across and fitted her safety belt before tending to his own.

'Taking you to a hotel.'

Her face lit with scandalised disbelief. 'No, you're not!' She leaned forward. 'Driver, take me to Applecross.' She supplied the street address, and caught a glimpse of familiar features in the rear-vision mirror and was unable to hide her disbelief. 'Carlo?'

'I'm sorry. I have orders.'

Shannay turned towards Marcello and lashed out at him with her hand, uncaring where it landed…as long as it did.

Except he caught it mid-flight, and pressed their joined hands down to his side.

'Nicki is asleep, Anna is happy to stay with her overnight, and there's a bag containing a change of clothes in the boot.'

He'd already been to the apartment?

'Why?'

'I imagine it's self-explanatory,' Marcello drawled, and she curled her fingers into his, then dug her nails in hard.

'You can't *do* this.'

She caught a flash of white teeth as he smiled in the dim light. 'So—bite me.'

She wanted to, badly. And she would, the instant they were alone. Meantime she refused to speak to him, or even look at him during the drive into the city.

Carlo pulled into the entrance of one of the city's luxurious hotels, popped the boot, retrieved two overnight bags and handed them to the hovering concierge.

'I'll call you in the morning,' Marcello indicated as Carlo opened the rear passenger door for Shannay to alight.

For a moment she considered refusing to budge, except making a fuss would gain nothing at all.

'I hate you for this.' Her voice was little more than a sibilant whisper as he led her through the foyer to a bank of lifts.

'Let go my hand,' Shannay demanded tightly when they alighted on a high floor.

'Soon.'

He was taller, and indisputably faster on his feet...so where did he think she'd escape to? She threw him a dark look and stood in mutinous silence as he inserted the card, freed the lock, then drew her inside.

With economical movements he deposited both bags, removed the *do not disturb* tag and hung it outside the door, then closed the door and slid home the safety chain.

'You'd better have a good reason for behaving like a...' Words temporarily failed her. 'Barbaric beast,' she added with considerable heat.

He was too controlled, his eyes too impossibly dark, except she was too angry to heed their caution.

'Why don't you sit down?'

'I don't *need* to sit.'

Marcello shrugged out of his leather jacket and threw it over the back of a nearby chair.

'A drink? A cup of tea, perhaps?'

He was being too polite, and she sent him a venomous glare. 'Cut to the chase, why don't you?'

'Then you can leave?' His drawling voice resembled pure silk being razzed by a sharp steel blade. 'I don't think so.'

'What is this?' Her dark eyes flashed with latent fire. 'A duel to the death?'

He smiled, although there was a distinct lack of humour apparent. 'You possess a fanciful imagination.'

Her chin lifted in open defiance. 'You're holding me here against my will.'

Marcello regarded her steadily, his gaze that of a jungle animal watching its prey. 'Are you pregnant with my child?'

Shannay was suddenly speechless, and it took several seconds before she found her voice. 'You flew from Madrid to ask that of me?'

'If you recall,' he drawled with silky indolence, 'you refused to give me an answer on the phone.'

Angry beyond belief, she searched for words, any words. 'You're *unbelievable*.'

'You're evading the question.' His voice assumed the quality of silk, and her features became waxen-pale.

'What if I say *no?*'

'It won't make the slightest difference.'

'To *what?*' she demanded, almost at the end of her tether.

'How this plays out.'

So this was it…crunch time.

'In a matter of weeks the divorce will be finalised.'

'No, it won't. I've had my lawyer notify yours of our reconciliation,' Marcello informed and obtained a degree of satisfaction at her shocked expression. 'Copies of the announcement in the Spanish media provided sufficient proof.'

'But that was merely a sham,' Shannay protested, eyes

wide with dismay as she searched frantically for the exact words quoted...hadn't Marcello simply acceded "anything is possible"? How could that be construed to be a positive confirmation?

She watched with startled surprise as he reached for his overnight bag, extracted a slim packet, opened the flap and handed the contents to her.

'I'd like you to look at these.'

Shannay told herself she wasn't interested, but the coloured photograph of a house caught her attention, and she felt herself drawn to it, unable to ignore her admiration for the beautiful, sprawling two-storeyed mansion set in spacious grounds overlooking what appeared to be a lake.

Underneath the photograph was another, even more magnificent, and there was a third with views out over the ocean.

Yet it was the first photograph she returned to, and she glanced up at him with open curiosity.

'Why are you showing me these?'

'The first house is at Peppermint Grove, the remaining two at Cottesloe and Cottesloe Beach respectively.'

Expensive real estate. *Very* expensive real estate, she perceived.

'We have an appointment to inspect them tomorrow.'

A soundless gasp escaped her lips. 'Excuse me?'

'You heard.'

She had, but the implication of them failed to compute. Why would he be interested in Perth real estate?

He watched her conflicting emotions and barely restrained himself from hauling her into his arms.

The past few weeks had been hell. He'd eaten at his desk, barely slept and literally turned his life upside down as he had liaised with Perth real-estate agents, selected three of the most suitable properties after viewing them via an internet visual tour, then he'd flown into Perth yesterday, consulted with lawyers, accountants, viewed the three properties and a few more purported to be worthy of inspection, organised Nicki's care with Anna…and had Carlo drive him to collect the reason for all this.

Shannay.

'We can do this by arguing half the night away,' Marcello began with deliberate patience. 'Or you can listen until I'm done.'

She looked at him, really looked at him, and saw the fine lines of tiredness fan out from each corner of his eyes, the faint shadowy smudges evident.

Heaven knew she was weary as pregnancy took hold of her body and drained some of her energy to nurture the tiny foetus developing inside her womb.

Together, what hope did they have?

Yet there was an instinctive feeling…some deep intrinsic knowledge hovering just beneath the surface.

His presence here…dared she even hope, let alone think what it might mean?

It was crazy, but the stress and tension that had consumed her for the past few weeks began to ebb, as if her subconscious recognised something she had yet to acknowledge.

Dared not envisage in case she might have it wrong.

'You have my heart, *querida*.'

For a few seconds she almost forgot to breathe.

'Always,' Marcello added gently. 'There has never been anyone else since the day I met you.'

She opened her mouth, only to close it again as he held up a hand.

'Please…hear me out. There are words I need to say. Not all of them good.'

She had nothing to lose. Absolutely nothing, and she simply inclined her head.

'Penè made things difficult for you, conspiring initially with Estella to cause trouble.'

Wasn't that the truth!

'I thought we could get beyond the resulting fracas, but you were adamant our marriage was doomed.'

'I left, because to remain would have been impossible.'

'I was angry,' Marcello continued. 'You ignored my phone calls and refused to respond to every one of my messages. Within a year Ramon developed pneumonia and suffered a heart attack. Soon after he was diagnosed with cancer, and it was necessary for me to take control.'

Marcello's responsibility would have been enormous. Remorse and a degree of guilt sat uncomfortably on her shoulders.

Timing, distance, misunderstanding. Each rational in hindsight, Shannay admitted.

'With your refusal to acknowledge any form of contact, I had little recourse but to accept you intended to make a life on your own.' He paused, and a muscle tensed along the edge of his jaw. 'Until fate played a hand with Sandro and Luisa's impromptu visit to Perth, their sighting of you at a local carnival and the discovery you had a child. Indisputably my child.'

Shannay relived that moment as if it were yesterday. 'I vowed revenge. Contriving to use everything in my power to have you revisit Madrid…and ultimately seduce you. To take hold of your emotions and crush them to dust beneath my feet.'

The knowledge sent pain arrowing through her body, and his voice softened as he glimpsed the shadows evident in her eyes.

'Except I couldn't do it. The woman I'd turned you into in my mind didn't exist. The reality was the young woman I fell in love with, the beautiful girl with integrity and a loving heart who fought against me and her own emotions…as I struggled to deal with my own.'

His mouth twisted with deliberate cynicism. 'Ironic, isn't it? When it came to revenge…I lost. As Ramon warned I would.'

Her eyes sharpened. 'Ramon?'

'My grandfather saw more than anyone gave him credit for. He'd glimpsed what was in your heart, and knew my own.'

What came next was painful. 'Nicki's abduction became the catalyst. I only had myself to offer in a bid to keep you with me.' He lifted a hand and let it fall to his side. 'And it wasn't enough.'

In his eyes, he'd failed yet again, and her sense of remorse returned.

'I didn't want Nicki to grow up shadowed by bodyguards, forever in fear of another abduction attempt.'

'Nor is it my choice,' he agreed quietly. 'Once is one time too many. Which brings me to my decision to relocate here.'

Shannay looked at him in disbelief. '*Perth?* How can you—'

'Easily. Sandro is now in control of the Madrid office. I've already signed a lease on suitable office accommodation in the city, and tomorrow we look at these houses.'

It was almost too much for her to take in. Yet any doubt fled as he took both her hands in his and lifted them to his lips.

'I love you,' he vowed gently. 'Stay with me, live with me. Let me love you, *mi mujer,* for the rest of my days. *Por siempre.*'

Forever.

They were only words, but they came from the heart, his soul…and were all she'd ever needed to hear.

Shannay withdrew her hands and cradled his face. Then she reached up, angled her mouth to his own and bestowed a lingering kiss.

'Yes,' she answered simply, and felt the tension ease from his body as he pulled her in close, then his mouth captured hers in a hungry, acutely sensual possession lasting long before he gradually eased to brush her swollen lips with his own, tracing their outline with a feather-light touch before lifting his head.

'I think this calls for a celebration.'

Marcello crossed to the phone and ordered a bottle of exceedingly expensive French champagne be sent up from the bar, and when it was delivered he eased off the cork and poured the sparkling, light golden liquid into two flutes and handed her one.

'To us.'

She lifted it and touched the rim to his own. Only to have her eyes widen in sudden consternation.

'What is it?'

'I—' there was never going to be a better time to tell him '—shouldn't have more than a sip of this,' she offered with obvious reluctance, and saw his eyes sharpen, then assume a lazy gleam.

'Because?' Marcello prompted gently, and glimpsed a mischievous smile teasing the corners of that lush mouth.

'It has to do with my being in the first trimester.'

She watched his expression change, and could only wonder at the joy, the love and an entire gamut of emotions flooding his features.

His eyes, she could die and go to heaven just on the look exposed there.

For her. Only her.

He laid the palm of one hand to her waist and splayed his fingers over her stomach.

'You don't mind?'

How could she mind?

She'd been fiercely protective of Nicki before and after she was born. Uncaring she'd chosen single motherhood over the alternative.

This time Marcello would be with her every step of the way.

'I'm delighted,' she assured gently.

'You gift me everything I could ever want, *amada*. All I need.'

The champagne went flat, which was total sacrilege.

Not that it mattered in the slightest, for there were more important matters to be taken care of.

Such as the leisurely removal of clothes, long, lingering kisses…and gentle tactile lovemaking far into the night.

CHAPTER THIRTEEN

IT WAS EARLY when Shannay woke, and she stretched, felt strong hands pull her in against a hard, warm, fully aroused male body, and gave a pleasurable sigh.

'Hmm,' she murmured as lips nuzzled the sensitive hollow at the curve of her neck. 'This is a very pleasant way to greet the morning.'

She reached for him, enclosed his hard length with light fingers, heard the faint hitch as the breath caught in his throat…and smiled.

'There's just one thing,' she began tentatively as Marcello's hand cupped her breast.

'And what's that?' he drawled close to her ear.

Oh, dear…not now, please. 'Morning sickness,' she enlightened as the nausea rose up in waves, and she made an undignified dash to the bathroom, clicked the lock, before being violently ill.

She barely registered the rattle of the door handle, and studiously ignored the double knock as Marcello demanded to be let in.

'I'm fine.'

The assurance didn't work, for she heard him utter a string of wicked-sounding Spanish imprecations. 'Open the door.'

'I'll be out in a minute.'

Not exactly an auspicious start to the day, and definitely not an enticing prelude to amorous activities, she grimaced as she washed her face and cleaned her teeth.

While there, she ran a brush through the tumbled length of her hair and twisted it into a knot atop her head, then she released the lock and emerged to find a concerned Marcello bent on dragging agitated fingers through badly rumpled hair.

A warm hand cupped her shoulder, while a firm thumb and finger captured her chin and lifted it as he subjected her to a dark-eyed scrutiny.

'Are you OK?'

Next he'll query if he should call a doctor…

He didn't disappoint, and he frowned as she rolled her eyes.

'What?'

'Morning sickness is a common occurrence during the early months of pregnancy,' she relayed with an impish grin. 'And not always confined to the morning.' She lifted a shoulder in a negligible shrug. 'It tends to wear off during the second trimester.'

'Is there nothing that helps?'

'Most often a cup of tea and a plain biscuit as soon as I wake will avert the physical symptoms.'

He crossed to the phone. 'I'll order Room Service.'

'Do that, for breakfast,' Shannay qualified. 'I'll make the tea.'

He looked appealingly disconcerted, and she had a difficult time hiding a smile.

Marcello Martinez, corporate head, entrepreneur and billionaire…master of many things, but a tad lost around his pregnant wife.

'I have a feeling I'm in for a learning curve,' he acknowledged with musing wryness.

She laughed, a low, throaty sound that was infectious. 'You'll do fine.' As he did with everything he chose to undertake.

He smoothed a hand over her cheek, cupped it, then traced her lower lip with his thumb. 'Starting now. Sit down and I'll make the tea.'

They showered, ate a leisurely breakfast, then checked out of the hotel and met Carlo, who drove them to Shannay's apartment in suburban Applecross, where Nicki greeted her father with unabashed affection.

'Daddy! Are you here for a visit?'

Shannay watched as Marcello swung their daughter into his arms and hugged her close.

'A very long visit.'

'Love you, Daddy.'

'Right back at you, *pequena*.'

Shannay swallowed the sudden lump in her throat at his smile.

'What would you say to me staying with you and Mummy?'

Nicki wound her arms around his neck and sank back in the cradle of his arms to regard him solemnly. 'Here, with us in Perth? All the time?'

'All the time,' he reiterated gently. 'Occasionally I'll need to visit Madrid, but I won't be away long, and sometimes you and Mummy can come with me.'

'I'd like it. Very much.' She leaned forward and kissed his cheek and assured plaintively, 'I missed you.'

'I missed you, too.'

It was enough knowing Marcello would be a permanent fixture for Nicki to go happily off to kindergarten while her parents met with real-estate agents.

The Peppermint Grove house won Shannay's vote. It was so *right* in every aspect, with its large grounds, spacious rooms and the most glorious curved staircase leading from an elegant tiled foyer to the upper floor.

All she needed to do was say "I love it", and Marcello closed the deal there and then.

Next came legal confirmation notification that the court would in all probability succeed in negating the processing of their decree absolute, thus voiding the existing divorce application.

The following few weeks proved hectic, as Shannay ordered furniture, furnishings and fittings, and, with Marcello organising delivery and placement, successfully orchestrated the move to their new home.

Shannay refused to leave John without a registered pharmacist, and worked a shorter evening shift for the week it took to employ a replacement.

Nicki loved her new bedroom, and delighted in the special playhouse Marcello had set up in the grounds for her.

By far, the baby news won out, with the future advent of a little sister or brother providing endless excitement.

Marcello was busy setting up a city office, employing staff and organising office space at home.

At his suggestion Shannay chose to lease her Applecross apartment, fortuitously to Anna's daughter and son-in-law, who had decided to relocate from Tasmania.

Everything seemed to fit into place with organised efficiency…mostly due to Marcello's influence, including a re-affirmation of their wedding vows to be held in the gardens of their Peppermint Grove home.

Sandro and Luisa flew in via private jet to attend the ceremony, while Penè declined on the grounds she was still mourning Ramon.

The day dawned with pale sunshine and a sky with drifting

cumulus, and caterers moved in mid-morning to prepare a sumptuous late-afternoon feast for the few guests Marcello and Shannay had chosen to invite.

It was the antithesis of the media circus their first wedding had become, and Nicki was in her element as Anna helped dress her in a miniature version of Shannay's gown. Wearing ivory shoes and a coronet of small flowers in her hair, she resembled a little princess.

Shannay chose a simple full-length gown in ivory silk with a long-sleeved slim-fitted jacket in matching fabric with a stand-up collar, ivory stilettos and a sheer scarf in ivory chiffon draped over her hair.

Her only jewellery was a diamond pendant and matching ear-studs.

There was an ornamental white gazebo in the grounds, decorated with white flowers, and Marcello stood resplendent in a dark suit, white shirt and ivory satin tie together with the celebrant as they waited for Shannay and Nicki to join them.

John and Anna acted as witnesses, and the vows were personally selected to endorse Shannay and Marcello's commitment to each other.

Guests were few, and consequently it was a very intimate gathering, with fine champagne, exquisite food, and much laughter.

Nicki was in her element, loving every minute of the day, and she made no protest when it came time for Carlo to take her with Anna for a sleep-over at Anna's apartment.

The caterers packed up, John departed, together with the remaining guests, and Sandro and Luisa left soon after for their city hotel.

Marcello closed and locked the door, then he drew

Shannay into his arms and touched his mouth to hers in a gentle salutation.

'Have I told you how beautiful you are?'

He had, when he'd slid her wedding ring in place, and again as the afternoon drew to a close.

A teasing smile curved her lips and she tilted her head slightly to one side. 'Should I commend how incredibly handsome you look?'

'Minx. Come dance with me, hmm?'

'That could lead to trouble.'

'Of the most delightful kind,' he agreed. 'But what's a wedding without a bridal waltz?'

She pressed a light kiss to his chin. 'Where?'

He activated a remote control and slow, dreamy music filtered through concealed speakers.

Together they barely moved, just held each other and drifted a little, swayed some, and Shannay felt boneless as the music crept into her soul, meshed with the overwhelming love she felt for the man who held her, and she rested against him, following wherever he led.

The track eventually concluded, and she pulled his head down to hers and kissed him.

'I love you.' The words drifted from her lips in a husky murmur. 'So much.' She thread her fingers through his hair, then caressed his nape, the sensitive skin beneath each earlobe, and rested against the pulse beating strongly at the base of his throat. 'I always have. Always will.'

He caught hold of her hand, unfolded it and laid his lips to her palm. *'Gracias.'*

She'd said the words before, but not quite like this, without accompanying passion, or in the dreamy aftermath of lovemaking.

'Let's go upstairs.'

Marcello placed a kiss to her forehead. 'Is that an invitation?'

'Do you need one?'

He placed an arm beneath her knees and lifted her into his arms, then began ascending the staircase.

'Isn't this just a little over the top?' she teased, and he chuckled.

'Perhaps I'm conserving your strength?'

'Next you'll suggest I lie supine while you do all the work.'

'It has been a long day.'

For which he received a thump on his arm from a very feminine fist.

'Wretch. Just as long as you remember I get to play payback in the early dawn hours.'

'Promises, huh?' They reached the main bedroom and he slid her down onto her feet, then they began removing each other's clothes…slowly, with infinite care.

Their love was everlasting, infinite and very special.

There was no need to hurry. They had the night, and all those remaining for the rest of their lifetimes.

Eternity.

Ramon Alejandro Martinez was born five months and two weeks later in the presence of his father, who cut the umbilical cord and handed him into his mother's arms.

With black hair, knowing eyes, he was the image of Marcello, and appeared to possess his mother's nature.

His sister, Nicki, adored him from first sight, and vowed to take care of him forever and teach him everything she knew.

Celebrate 100 years of pure reading pleasure with Mills & Boon®

To mark our centenary, each month we're publishing a special 100th Birthday Edition. These celebratory editions are packed with extra features and include a FREE bonus story.

Now that's worth celebrating!

4th January 2008

The Vanishing Viscountess by Diane Gaston
With FREE story The Mysterious Miss M
This award-winning tale of the Regency Underworld launched Diane Gaston's writing career.

1st February 2008

Cattle Rancher, Secret Son by Margaret Way
With FREE story His Heiress Wife
Margaret Way excels at rugged Outback heroes…

15th February 2008

Raintree: Inferno by Linda Howard
With FREE story Loving Evangeline
A double dose of Linda Howard's heady mix of passion and adventure.

Don't miss out! From February you'll have the chance to enter our fabulous monthly prize draw. See special 100th Birthday Editions for details.

www.millsandboon.co.uk

FREE!

4 Books
and a surprise gift!

We would like to take this opportunity to thank you for reading this Mills & Boon® book by offering you the chance to take FOUR more specially selected titles from the Modern™ series absolutely FREE! We're also making this offer to introduce you to the benefits of the Mills & Boon® Reader Service™—

- ★ **FREE home delivery**
- ★ **FREE gifts and competitions**
- ★ **FREE monthly Newsletter**
- ★ **Exclusive Reader Service offers**
- ★ **Books available before they're in the shops**

Accepting these FREE books and gift places you under no obligation to buy, you may cancel at any time, even after receiving your free shipment. Simply complete your details below and return the entire page to the address below. You don't even need a stamp!

YES! Please send me 4 free Modern books and a surprise gift. I understand that unless you hear from me, I will receive 6 superb new titles every month for just £2.99 each, postage and packing free. I am under no obligation to purchase any books and may cancel my subscription at any time. The free books and gift will be mine to keep in any case.

P8ZEF

Ms/Mrs/Miss/Mr ....Initials................................
                                                                BLOCK CAPITALS PLEASE
Surname..
Address..
....
....Postcode ....

Send this whole page to:
UK: FREEPOST CN8I, Croydon, CR9 3WZ

Offer valid in UK only and is not available to current Mills & Boon® Reader Service™ subscribers to this series. Overseas and Eire please write for details. We reserve the right to refuse an application and applicants must be aged 18 years or over. Only one application per household. Terms and prices subject to change without notice. Offer expires 3lst May 2008. As a result of this application, you may receive offers from Harlequin Mills & Boon and other carefully selected companies. If you would prefer not to share in this opportunity please write to The Data Manager, PO Box 676, Richmond. TW9 IWU.

Mills & Boon® is a registered trademark owned by Harlequin Mills & Boon Limited.
Modern™ is being used as a trademark. The Mills & Boon® Reader Service™ is being used as a trademark.